ETHAN'S VOICE

ETHAN'S VOICE

RACHEL CARTER

SCHOLASTIC

First published in the UK in 2013 by Scholastic Children's Books
An imprint of Scholastic Ltd
Euston House, 24 Eversholt Street
London, NW1 1DB, UK
Registered office: Westfield Road, Southam, Warwickshire, CV47 0RA
SCHOLASTIC and associated logos are trademarks and/
or registered trademarks of Scholastic Inc.

ISBN 978 1407 13550 2

A CIP catalogue record for this book
is available from the British Library.

Printed and bound by CPI Group (UK) Ltd, Croydon, CR0 4YY
Papers used by Scholastic Children's Books are made from wood
grown in sustainable forests.

1 3 5 7 9 10 8 6 4 2

www.scholastic.co.uk/zone

For everyone who needs a big breath
to make them brave.

CHAPTER 1

Ethan kicked off his muddy trainers and left them on the grass. The pond had been good this morning: he had caught minnows and three newts. He walked along the plank at the front of *Deity*, and stepped down on to the deck of the bow. The doors were wide open. A voice floated up from inside.

"How is Ethan?"

As he listened at the doorway, Ethan's heart raced. It was Mary from the council. It was her job to check Mum taught him his lessons properly, because he didn't go to school.

Ethan ducked his head and climbed down on to the first step and into *Deity*.

"Is he still reading a lot of books?"

Mary sat by the kitchen on the fold-out chair. Mum was in the lounge on the sofa. Dad sat next to her in his best jeans when he should have been at work. They all stopped talking when Ethan reached the last stair.

"Ethan," Mary smiled.

Dad's eyebrows pinched together. He nodded to the sofa. "Sit yourself down."

Ethan put his net on the floor by the window that looked out over the canal. Mum shuffled along so he could sit beside her.

"How was the pond?" asked Mary. "Catch anything?"

He nodded.

Mum was wearing the brown boots that she kept for town and the skirt she'd just finished making. She put her hand on Ethan's. "I was just saying how well you're doing," she said, smiling. "How you're starting a new history project."

"I'm glad." Mary crossed her legs and leant closer. "So, you've been reading all about knights for the last

2

couple of weeks?"

Ethan smiled.

"I hear your maths has come on, and your science. Are you finding enough reading books in the library?"

He nodded.

Mary fixed him with her twinkly eyes. "Are you happy being on the boat so much, Ethan?"

He nodded harder.

Mary tucked her hair behind her ear. "Do you get a little lonely when you're studying? You see, I had an idea."

What did Mary mean? She never asked these kinds of question.

Dad's forehead was creased with lines. It looked the same way when one of his gardening jobs got cancelled. Dad was biting his nails now and jigging his leg like he was nervous. Mum took a big breath.

"You're doing so well," said Mary, "I thought. . ."

Dad turned to Ethan and spoke fast like a gush of water. "We thought you could go back to school."

Ethan stood up. He was going to be sick. How could they surprise him like that?

"It's OK." Mum grabbed his hand. "Don't be upset."

The boat swayed. Ethan shook his head again and again. He wanted to shout NO! but he couldn't. He wanted to run up the bow stairs and back down the canal to the pond. He wanted to get away from all of them.

"Ethan, just sit down." Dad did a big sigh like he didn't know what to say. "We're just trying to help you."

"Sit down, Ethan. Please." Mum squeezed his hand tight. Her eyes were watery now like she might cry.

He sat. *Deity*'s walls closed in around him.

"Don't be frightened," said Dad.

"It was just an idea," said Mary. "I know it's been four years since you were at school. I know it wasn't easy with some of the other children after you stopped speaking." Ethan shivered. "It's bound to be a little scary."

Mum put her arm around Ethan. She smiled. "We could try a different school? We said being home taught wasn't for ever. It might help you."

"We don't want to . . . *hold you back* now that you're getting older," said Mary.

Ethan drew a sharp breath. He knew what Mary meant by holding him back. She wasn't talking about his schoolwork, because Mum always said how well he was doing. She meant being taught on the canal might stop him from ever speaking again, because Mum and Dad let him nod, or shake his head instead; because he wasn't around other children who would try to get him to speak and join in their games. He might miss out on lots of things, like having proper friends and one day getting a job that needed you to talk.

For a while, Mum had taken him to see a special man. The man had asked Ethan why he didn't talk any more, but Ethan couldn't tell him. Then Mum had taken him to a nice lady to play speaking games, but still the words wouldn't come out. Mum and Dad kept asking him lots of questions. Mum tried to get him to read his bedtime story out loud. Dad used to play the guitar to try to get Ethan to sing along. Sometimes Dad used to tickle him to try and make Ethan say stop. After a while, Mum and Dad had to stop asking questions that Ethan couldn't shake his head or nod to. They weren't sure what else to do.

"Go on, Mary," said Dad.

"I've spoken with Mr Cabot," said Mary. "He's the headmaster at Orchard School. It's a little further than your old school, but it's smaller. I could arrange a visit. You'd be in the oldest year group this time, now you're eleven. There wouldn't be any older boys. And we'd make sure the children didn't try to *make* you speak."

Ethan looked at the floor.

"Listen," said Dad. He sounded cross now. "This is important."

Ethan pushed the rug with his foot so it slid and he didn't have to look at them.

"We aren't going to *force* you to go to school," said Mary. "It has to be your decision."

Dad spoke quietly. "Do you think trying another school might help?"

"If Ethan's willing to give it a try," said Mary.

Mum looked at Ethan. She tried to smile. She turned back to Mary. "I think that's enough for now," she said.

"Of course," said Mary.

Mary finished her coffee. She stood and put her cup on the kitchen countertop.

"I'll come back in a few weeks, Ethan. Just have a little *think* about school for me."

She took her coat from the back of the chair. Mum and Dad followed her up the bow stairs. He could hear them on the towpath: Mary talking about how school could help him speak again. How the other children would be made to understand. He could hear Dad saying how he didn't know what to do for the best. How they should try everything.

Ethan's head swirled. He padded through the lounge and the kitchen, past the bathroom to his cabin at the back of *Deity*, through the engine room. Ethan opened his cabin door and turned the catch at the top of the cupboard so his bed unfolded. He lay back and said it over and over in his head: *school, school, school*.

It wouldn't matter if he was the eldest. The boys his age could still pick on him because he didn't talk, like the older boys had, before. When they had found out he had stopped talking, three of them tugged his hair to try and make him talk when the lunch lady wasn't about. They pretended it was funny at first. Then they called him mean names and kicked him and he had cried, but still he hadn't spoken. He couldn't.

Once, the lunch lady had seen the boys picking on him and told their teacher, but the boys still called him names when no one was looking. Then, one morning, after the boys had taken his jumper the day before and thrown it up a tree, Ethan wouldn't come out of his cabin to go to school. He cut up his uniform with the scissors and Mum had cried and Dad had shouted "Enough", and they all went to see the headmaster. When they got home Mum and Dad sat Ethan on the sofa and Mum said she'd teach him on the boat, "For Now".

He was meant to go to another school, one day. But he worked really hard to get all his answers right so he could stay at home. And Mum and Dad stopped talking about real school. And Mary came to see him and Mum said he was doing "better than ever", and they never mentioned real school. But being at home hadn't helped him to speak again. It had been so long since he had spoken that he couldn't remember how it felt, or why he had stopped. It was like he had always been this way.

Mum came into his cabin when Mary had gone. She knelt by the bed. Her ponytail was falling out.

She stroked Ethan's forehead with her fingers. "We didn't mean to startle you," she said.

Ethan grabbed his stack of knight books from the floor. He was still angry with Mum and Dad. He lay back and opened his favourite book: *Life of a Knight*. He stared down at the title of the first chapter: "Becoming a Knight".

Mum didn't say anything else.

"Starting that project now?" Dad spoke quietly as he poked his head around the door. "You'll have to show me sometime."

Ethan didn't nod. He reached for the laptop under the bed. He turned it on and opened a new document. His project was going to be a knight's journal. He'd start his journal as if he were a page: a boy sent to a castle to learn how to become a knight.

Dad should understand. Mum said he was teased for being a boater when he was young. But Dad never talked about it. That was why Dad had left school early. That was why he didn't like it when new people took to canal life. Dad said he didn't trust newcomers very often.

Ethan started to type. His page hated the castle. He couldn't even shoot a straight arrow because his hands shook when he pulled back his bow. The other pages teased him for it. He didn't think he'd ever become a knight and make his father proud.

"Just think about school," said Mum. She got up and left the cabin.

It didn't matter what Mary said, or Mum, or even Dad.

He'd never go back to school.

CHAPTER 2

Ethan put his breakfast plate in the washing-up bowl. Dad sat quietly at the table sipping his coffee. Dad hadn't spoken about school this morning. His gardening job had been cancelled and his forehead was etched with lines again.

"Hope it doesn't rain." Mum was at the countertop folding skirts she had made for the market. Next to her was a box of jugs she'd painted.

Merlin sat on the floor at Mum's feet. She meowed when she saw Ethan.

Dad got up and pressed his face to the window that looked east over the water.

"Holiday-makers," Dad tutted. "They're mooring their flash new boat on the pound." He turned to Mum. "I told you, the canal's changing."

Mum rolled her eyes. She went over to the window and looked out. "Don't worry about that," she said. "They'll be gone soon."

Ethan was surprised. A new boat on the pound? This hardly ever happened. Boats passed by, but they rarely stopped. *Deity* was the only boat that was always moored on the pound.

Before Mum and Dad had got married, Dad and Gran lived on *Deity*. When she died, Gran had made Dad promise that he would never sell *Deity* and never stop being a boater, because her family had lived on the water for generations. Dad said he was proud that *Deity* was so old. But Ethan had caught Dad on the laptop, looking at big new boats like the one he had called "flash".

"Can you get that box, Jake?" said Mum. "We're going to be late."

Dad lifted the box of jugs and took the van keys from the sideboard.

"We need to set up the stall, Ethan," said Mum. "I've left you my mobile and Dad will be back in a bit, OK? Do the next chapter of your science book and your maths. Then carry on with your knight project; we'll have a lesson when I'm back."

Ethan nodded.

"Take the rubbish out for me, son." Dad nodded at the black bag by the countertop. He smiled but his eyes didn't shine. If Dad was helping Mum, that meant he didn't have any gardening jobs booked in for this afternoon either.

Dad said he'd have to drive lorries if the business didn't pick up. That meant he'd have to get up really early and he wouldn't get back till late at night. Ethan would hardly see him. And if Dad didn't get more gardening jobs, Mum would have to find work that was better paid than the market stall, but Dad said he wouldn't let it come to that. Ethan hoped not. He couldn't stay on *Deity* by himself if Mum and Dad were at work all day.

Mum and Dad climbed the front stairs and shut the bow doors. Ethan went to the same window Dad had looked out of. It was a grey, misty day. The new boat was moored three boat-lengths away with its wide stern facing *Deity*'s bow. The boat was blue, bright blue against the dreary sky. It had a matching blue railing that curved around the stern like a horseshoe. Its stern doors were the colour of honey. The blacking around the bottom was so new that it gleamed.

It was the most beautiful boat Ethan had ever seen.

He was about to come away from the window when the blue boat's stern doors opened. A red figure climbed out on to the stern deck. It was a girl in a red coat. She had long black hair. She looked down the canal to *Deity*. Ethan flinched and pulled back from the window. He waited a little, then slowly drew his face back up to the glass. The girl walked along the stern deck to the horseshoe-shaped railing. She folded her arms over the railing and leant closer to the water. She kept leaning until her feet lifted off the deck, and she stayed like that for a while, just staring down at the water, her feet swinging to and fro in the air, like her head was heavy with thinking.

The girl dropped her feet to the floor and backed away from the railing. She was in the middle of the stern deck now, with her arms stretched out. She began to spin around and around. She was dancing, smiling. Her head dropped back and she stared up at the sky.

The girl began to slow. She wobbled a little as she stopped twirling. She laughed, and then she took her eyes from the sky and looked right at Ethan's window.

Ethan flinched.

Did she see me?

The girl waved and smiled. She turned away. She skipped back to the stern doors and climbed into the boat.

She saw me!

The doors shut.

Ethan watched the empty stern for while.

He stepped away from the window.

Ethan stared down at the bag of rubbish by the countertop. He'd done his maths. Dad might be back from the market soon. He'd better take the rubbish out. Dad wouldn't understand why the girl on the blue boat made Ethan afraid to go down the canal.

Ethan went to the window. There wasn't any sign of the girl. The dump shed was just a few metres from *Deity* towards the blue boat. He'd be really quick, in case the girl came out. Then he'd come back and do his science chapter.

Ethan got his fleece from his cabin. He lifted the bag of rubbish and climbed the stairs to the bow. He pushed back the doors. The cold air nibbled his nose and fingers as he climbed out on to the deck. He looked down the canal to check the girl was still inside. It was safe. He took a big breath.

The plank from the bow to the bank was slippery with frost. The grass was tipped ghosty-white. There were shiny frozen puddles in the dips near the towpath. Ethan walked as fast as he could, but the bag was heavy.

He passed the tree where Dad had tied up the hammock to surprise Mum last summer. Dad was good at surprises and building things. He had built Ethan an amazing sledge when it was snowy last year, and a big run for the rabbit he used to have. But Dad only seemed to think about the business right now.

Ethan turned away from the canal path to the dump shed. It was just a few more steps to the dump-shed door. Then he slid back the bolt and swung the bag inside.

Crack! Ethan jumped. He turned to face the canal.

It was the girl in the red coat. He'd been too busy thinking about Dad to notice her. She was jumping on a frozen puddle near the stern of her boat. She wore blue wellies with green spots. The ice on the puddle cracked; there was a splash. She looked up and saw him.

"I did it." The girl smiled like she had when she was dancing on her boat. "I need another one now." She stepped out of the icy puddle and on to the towpath. "Not that one, it's too pretty," she said.

Ethan hurried back to *Deity*. He didn't turn around.

In the lounge he peeped out of the window and looked east down the water. He couldn't see the girl on the towpath. She'd gone.

Ethan had just finished his science when the Mum's mobile rang. He saw it was Dad on the display and pressed the answer button.

"I'm staying to help Mum run the stalls," said Dad. "Hope your work's gone OK. See you later, son."

Ethan hung up. He'd read his knight book in peace for a bit, and then he would do his journal. He found the book on the floor of his cabin. He climbed up the cabin steps and out of the little double doors, on to the deck of *Deity's* stern. Ethan shut the cabin doors and sat against them, pulling up his knees to get comfy. He looked out over the back of the boat and down the canal. This was the best place to sit, looking west over the water. There weren't any blue boats moored down this end of the canal.

Ethan opened *Life of a Knight*. He started reading all about the Knight's Code. How a knight had to speak the truth at all times and do the right thing, even if that made the knight unhappy. How knights defended those who could not defend themselves.

"Hello?"

Ethan put down the book. He froze for a moment, just listening. Someone was coming down the towpath; he could hear their footsteps. He shuffled to the left of the stern deck so he was closer to the canal bank. He ducked his head around the left side of *Deity's* stern so that he could see who was coming. It was the girl in the red coat; she was only a few steps away from him. His heart started to beat fast. But it was OK; she hadn't seen him yet.

Ethan shuffled to the right of the deck so he was

closer to the cabin doors. He quickly made a plan. He'd turn around and open the doors and get inside fast, before she saw him.

"Why are you hiding?" The girl was on the bank beside Ethan. It was too late. She was already there and she was waiting for him to speak. He just wouldn't look at her. He'd look out over the water, like she wasn't there. He'd stare at the moorhens bobbing on the canal. Then she might leave.

"You've got a little dinghy." She pointed to the dingy that was tied to the right of *Deity's* stern.

"I dropped our boat hook," she said quietly. She smiled. "It's floating on the canal, but I can't reach it, it's too far out. Could you help me?" She looked at him silently for a moment. She didn't leave.

He shook his head. Why was she bothering him?

"How long have you lived on the canal?" she asked.

He didn't say anything. How could he?

She waited for his answer, but she didn't seem to mind when he didn't reply.

"It's lovely here," she carried on. "You saw me spinning on my boat."

It was hard to keep staring ahead. The girl was still there, watching, waiting for him to speak.

"Are you going to help me?"

Ethan's legs ached from sitting too long. He could climb back in his cabin but that would be rude.

"It won't take long," she said.

He looked at the girl. Her hair was as dark as a moorhen. Her nose turned up at the end. For just a second Ethan didn't look away.

"I don't think you like speaking," the girl said gently. She gazed at him for a while. "That doesn't matter."

Ethan's legs twisted with cramp. He stood up, but kept staring out at the water.

The girl clapped her hands. "Brilliant. You're coming."

His head began to spin. That wasn't meant to happen. Now the girl thought he was going to help her.

Ethan didn't move.

"This way." She started to walk down the towpath. She turned back and beckoned him. He stayed still. Her smile dropped. Her forehead scrunched up. She looked sad, like she had staring out at the water.

"Are you coming?"

Ethan didn't know what to do now. He didn't want

to go with the girl, but she looked so disappointed. It was like he had no choice.

"If you help me, you don't have to say anything." She smiled. "Don't be scared."

She didn't *seem* like she would tease him. But still, Ethan was afraid. He looked at the book in his hand and remembered that knights defended people who couldn't defend themselves. Knights helped others. But could *he* help the girl? She said he didn't have to speak. Maybe she understood.

Ethan turned around and eased *Deity*'s boat hook off the roof by grabbing the pole and inching it down over his cabin doors.

Slowly, Ethan walked along the plank on to the bank, his stomach tight. He wouldn't be with her for long. He'd make sure of it. He'd get her hook as fast as he could, and then he would head back to *Deity* and his knight book.

The girl started walking and Ethan followed.

"We're new to the canal," she said over her shoulder. "It's just me and Mum now. Mum's gone for milk."

He nodded. His heart thumped with each step.

"I've left my school. I'm having time off until we

find a permanent mooring to settle on. We won't be here for long. Do you go to school?"

Ethan shivered and shook his head.

"Are you taught on your boat?"

He nodded, but kept his eyes on the towpath ahead.

"Here we are."

Her boat was even more beautiful up close. There were metal flakes in the blue paint and they shone when they caught the light. On the side it said *Moon's End* in twirling yellow letters.

"The hook's down there." She pointed to the left of the stern.

It was floating on the water about two metres away from the bank. He would have to use his boat hook to pull it closer.

Ethan knelt down to the water and leant out. Slowly, he got hold of the floating pole with his boat hook, then, carefully, he pulled it towards to the bank. When the pole was close enough, he reached out with his spare hand and grabbed it, lifting it into the air with a shower of drops.

The girl took the hook and smiled. "Thank you," she said.

Ethan wiped his hands on his cords and looked down at the ground.

"I'm Polly," she said. Her skin was white. Her eyes were green like a cat's. Like his cat, Merlin.

He nodded and started back down the canal.

For a second, he wanted to turn back and say, "I'm Ethan," but he'd kept his words inside for too long. He didn't know how they would ever come out again.

Ethan put his boat hook on *Deity*'s roof. He found *Life of a Knight* on the deck of the stern and stepped down into his cabin. He unfolded his bed and turned on the laptop. He was ready to write his second journal entry now.

The words came fast. His page had met the lady of the castle; he'd found her comb in the moat and she'd smiled at him. She said her name was Isabel. The page wished he was a brave knight so he knew how to speak courteously and win her favour.

Ethan stared at the words on the screen. He was good at writing stories. He could always find the words for stories. So why couldn't he say them out loud?

Ethan was saving his entry when Mum and Dad got back.

Mum came into his cabin. "How's it going?" she asked. She sat next to him and marked his science and maths.

"All your answers were right," she said. "Now, let's see this knight project."

Ethan passed Mum the laptop. His breath quickened as she read.

"Ethan." Mum smiled and her eyes danced. "This is such a good idea. I want you to keep going. I'll read it all when it's done."

Dad smiled at Ethan over dinner. "You did some good journal writing today, then?"

Ethan nodded.

"I'll have to take a look sometime."

Ethan sat very still.

"Ethan?" said Dad.

He didn't move. He looked at Mum. He wasn't sure Dad would understand the journal. What if he teased him about Isabel?

"What do you think?" said Dad. But still, Ethan didn't nod.

Dad let out a sigh. He finished his food and pushed his plate away.

"He's only just started it, Jake," said Mum. "Maybe have a look when it's finished."

Dad gave a small shrug. He stood up and took his coat from the hook.

"I'm going for a cigarette," he said.

Mum reached out and held Ethan's hand. "He's worried about the business, that's all." She spoke softly. "And he wants to *help* you."

CHAPTER 3

That night, Ethan dreamt about the girl from the blue boat. Polly. He didn't want to think about her, but he couldn't help it. She was trapped inside his head, like a butterfly in a jam jar.

He knew it was just a dream because every now and then Merlin padded over his chest, her claws catching on his quilt. Then Ethan slipped far away, tugged back to his Polly dream.

Ethan was a knight in his dream, but he didn't have a sword or any armour. Polly stood next to him on the towpath. "It's OK, I want to be your friend," she said. He wanted to run back to *Deity*, but his feet wouldn't move. She reached out and gave him a big sword. "To make you brave." She smiled. "One day you'll get your armour, like a real knight. One day you'll speak again. I can help you, if you let me?"

Gently, Polly tugged a red ribbon from his mouth. It scratched the top of his tongue, but she kept tugging and tugging. The ribbon stopped scratching and just tickled. Then there wasn't any ribbon left in his mouth and with a flick of Polly's wrist it rose into the sky and spiralled down into the water.

Ethan heard a meow. He opened his eyes and sat up. He was in bed. The dream had finished, but his heart was still racing. It was dark in his cabin. He turned on his lamp. His bedside clock said seven thirty a.m. Merlin jumped on his bed. Ethan heard a tap. He flinched. There was another tap. The taps were getting louder. They were coming from the window, opposite his bed, next to the bank. Someone was knocking on the glass. It must be Mum leaving to set up the market stall.

Slowly, Ethan sat up. He slid back the curtain. But

it wasn't Mum, or even Dad. It was Polly. He took a big breath.

Polly called out, "Open the window."

He stared at her. Why had she come?

She shook her head and laughed. "You need to open the window."

Ethan didn't move. His head was still full of the dream. Was he awake?

Polly pointed to the catch above the glass. She had freckles on her nose. "Please," she mouthed.

He could do it easily; he could just open the window.

Polly wasn't like the girls he'd met at school. She didn't seem like anyone he'd ever met. Maybe the dream had been true? Maybe she really wanted to be his friend?

Ethan slowly reached up and tugged the catch.

He opened the window towards him, just a little. His face flushed hot. Polly pressed her hand against the glass and the window opened wider. She had coloured beads on her wrist. Her hand was small.

Polly bent down. When she stood up she held a white box and she slid it through the window. Ethan smelt a sweet, buttery smell.

"I made you these," said Polly. "Take them."

The box was warm. Polly took her hands away. "They're really delicious."

"Ethan," she said, "that's your name." She was looking at the row of coloured letters hanging on the wall.

He nodded and smiled.

"Do you ever speak, Ethan?"

He shook his head.

"That's OK. I don't mind."

He looked down at the box in his hand. No one had ever come to his window with a present before, not even Dad. It wasn't even his birthday or Christmas. Polly had brought him a gift just because she wanted to.

"Buttermilk pancakes!" Polly smiled. "Enjoy them." She swung her back to the window and disappeared down the towpath.

Ethan knelt back on his bed with the box in his lap. Polly knew he didn't speak. She said she didn't mind. And she hadn't acted like he was strange. Merlin jumped up and nuzzled him. Dad didn't believe in taking gifts from strangers and he didn't like holidaymakers on the canal. Polly was a stranger and a holidaymaker. But she'd been really nice to him.

The bottom of the box warmed the top of Ethan's legs and the sweet smell filled his cabin. Soon, whatever was inside might be cold. He lifted the lid and breathed a waft of sweet air. It was a pile of golden circles: a little stack of pancakes. He counted them: six. They didn't look like Mum's pancakes. They were thicker and smaller: the size of his hand when he stretched out his fingers. Instead of sugar on the top there was a pool of golden liquid trickling down the sides.

Ethan dipped his finger in the golden pool and pressed the top pancake – it was springy, spongy. He lifted his finger to his lips and licked it. He peeled a pancake from the pile and bit in, coating his mouth in a syrupy stickiness. Then he saw a little scroll of paper tied up with a red ribbon. It had been tucked behind the pile of pancakes. He lifted the scroll and unrolled it.

Polly had written him a note.

COME TO MY BOAT.
TONIGHT, FOR HALLOWEEN.
AT MIDNIGHT.

Ethan stared at the words as he ate another pancake. Polly wanted him to go to her boat. For Halloween. Tonight. He couldn't, even if he wasn't shy with strangers. Dad would never let him stay up that late. And Dad wouldn't let him go to a newcomer's boat without meeting them first.

But I want to go to Polly's boat.

Other boats might pass by, but even if there were children on board, they wouldn't be like Polly. She said it didn't matter that he didn't talk. She'd brought him a surprise present. She wanted to be his friend, just the way he was.

Ethan finished his third pancake and licked his fingers. There were three pancakes left for later. He rolled up the piece of paper, tied the ribbon around it and put it in his secret drawer. He got washed and dressed and hid the box in his wardrobe. He shut up his fold-down bed.

Mum had already left for the market as he'd thought and Dad had work today. There was a note from Mum on the countertop.

Do the next chapter in your
science book, love.

Back in half an hour.
We'll have a lesson then.

Ethan sat on the stern deck with his back against his cabin doors and his science book in his lap. He wrote the answers in the empty spaces and tried to forget about Polly's note, but the words kept fluttering around inside his head.

TONIGHT, FOR HALLOWEEN

Ethan looked out over the water. Polly was coming towards him down the towpath. He was glad. She was wearing a green hat and swinging a plastic bag. She must have walked to the little shop at the west end of the canal.

"Hello!" she called out. "Were my pancakes lovely?"

Ethan nodded.

"I told you," Polly laughed.

Polly stopped at the side of the stern.

"Did you see the note?"

He nodded again.

"You're doing schoolwork. What subject?"

33

He held up his science book.

Polly wrinkled her nose. "Literacy's my favourite subject."

Mine too.

"I love reading."

Me too.

"I hope you can come tonight, to Halloween." Polly nodded to her shopping bag. "I'm making tons of food."

I can't.

Polly frowned. She spoke softly.

"Halloween's one of my favourite days, but it's the first year Dad won't be with us and he loves it too. It was Mum's idea to leave home. Dad's two hours away now."

Ethan needed to shake his head, to tell her he wouldn't be able to come, but he didn't. He didn't do anything.

Polly looked over at the water. When she looked back, her eyes glistened with tears. She sat on *Deity's* plank. She leant closer. "Can I tell you an awful secret?" she said, her voice was almost a whisper. "I haven't spoken to my dad since we left home a week ago. I said I'd call him, but I haven't. He's called Mum's phone, but I haven't called him back. I'm scared he'll sound really upset. I'm scared I'll be upset. Mum thinks I already called him."

She smiled just a little. Her eyes looked carefully at his. "Now I let my secret out."

Ethan stared at her. Polly had a secret and she'd shared it with him. No one had ever told him their secret before.

"Have you always lived on the water, Ethan?"

He nodded.

"I thought so."

"Have you ever been to school?"

He nodded and his head started to swim.

"I don't think you liked it," said Polly. "Don't be scared of coming to *Moon's End*. We won't try and make you talk. You'll come." Polly made it sound like it was true, but it couldn't be. "Won't you?"

What would a brave knight do? Ethan knew the answer straight away. He nodded. He couldn't help it. He wanted to go to Polly's boat, even though he wasn't allowed. If he didn't, she might never ask him again.

Did *Moon's End* smell of burnt wood, like *Deity*? Did Polly fold out her bed every night? Was there a hole in her cabin roof where the rain dripped through?

If Polly was his friend, they could explore the canal together. He could take her fishing on the pond. They could go over the bridge to the wood. He could show Polly his cabin. Ethan smiled as he thought about it. Mum and Dad might be really glad he'd made a friend; they might forget all about school.

"Brilliant. It'll be really good fun." Polly laughed and her eyes danced.

It made Ethan's hands tingle with nerves just thinking about going to *Moon's End*.

Polly stood up. "I've got to go. I'm making a cake for tonight. Then I'm going to have a little sleep so I can stay up late. You better finish your science."

Ethan ducked his head around the side of *Deity*'s stern and watched her go.

Polly turned back and waved. "See you at midnight, Ethan," she said.

CHAPTER 4

Ethan didn't feel very hungry at dinner. His heart started to flutter as he helped Dad clear the plates.

While Dad did the dishes and Mum took a shower, Ethan looked out of the lounge window. He took a deep breath. There were coloured lanterns all around *Moon's End*'s stern. He blinked but they were still there.

At bedtime Ethan ate the cold pancakes from the box in the wardrobe. They still tasted delicious. He put on his pyjamas and turned the catch at the top of the tall cupboard. His bed unfolded. He got under his quilt and turned out the lamp.

He listened for the sounds that meant Mum and Dad were going to bed: Dad in the bathroom, running the tap and noisily splashing water on his face like he did each night. Then the whirl of Mum's electric toothbrush, which seemed to go on for ever, and at last, the pull of the bathroom light cord when they'd both finished. Ethan heard the squeak as they made up the sofa bed to sleep. Then it all went quiet.

Ethan wriggled, trying to get comfortable. He turned on the lamp. He looked at his watch. It was eleven forty-five p.m now. It was time to go to Polly's boat, just like he'd promised. He was nervous and excited all mixed up together. He'd never sneaked out of *Deity* at night-time, but now he had to be brave.

He got out of bed and found a fleece, his cords and some old trainers on the floor. He took the torch from the hook beside his bed and flicked the switch. The light shone on the white castle on his wardrobe door and Ethan touched it for luck. He opened the secret drawer and took out Polly's note and read it. Polly really did want to be his friend. Ethan zipped the note in his fleece pocket.

He slid open the hatch in the roof, slowly, so it didn't make the scratchy noise that might wake Mum and Dad. He opened the stern doors and the cold crept inside. His hands shook. He shone the torch on the deck, took a big breath to make him brave and stepped out.

He was standing on the deck in the darkest dark. When he knelt down and felt for the plank to the left of the stern, it was still there; Dad must have forgotten to take it up for the night. Ethan took tiny steps so he didn't fall; then he dropped down, off the plank and on to the towpath. He turned left and crept away from his cabin, past the lounge where Mum and Dad were fast asleep. For a second he thought about turning back, but he walked on.

In the daytime the canal was at the middle of everything. Now the water was the same colour as the sky, blue-black like the ink in Mum's special pen. He couldn't tell the sky from the water. When he looked back, he couldn't see the stile that you climbed over to get to the pond. But he could see the white bridge up ahead, hanging over the water like a ghost.

There wasn't any noise from boats or people. Even the ducks were sleeping. The moon shone down on the water like silver foil.

This was his night.

The lanterns hung from *Moon's End*. Pink, yellow, blue and purple. They made circles of coloured light on the water.

Ethan took another big breath. He shone his torch at Polly's boat and walked closer.

Soon he was standing on the deck of *Moon's End*'s bow. His hand was trembling. There were candles at his feet and pots of flowers. The bow doors were shut; there wasn't any sign of Polly or her mum. Was he too late? Should he go back to *Deity*?

Then he saw it, sitting on the top of *Moon's End*, just above the bow doors. An orange head with diamond-shaped eyes and a toothy grin. A pumpkin lantern. It was staring right at him. It was glowing with fire. Ethan blinked, but the head was still there. He couldn't look away.

The bow doors swung open and he jumped.

"You're here!" A black figure climbed out of the boat and on to the bow deck.

"It's me, Polly," it said. "Come in." Polly wore a

black cat mask, dark trousers and a dark jumper. Her cat eyes shone greener than ever. She held open the door and beckoned him in. He glanced again at the pumpkin lantern and followed her, slowly stepping down on to a wooden box and into *Moon's End*, his breathing quick.

Moon's End was much wider than his boat. There weren't any lights, just candles hung from the ceiling in little glass holders. In the middle of the lounge was a dark wooden table with a big bowl of apples on top of it. Polly walked over to a big white sofa by the window next to the water.

"Time for apple bobbing!" A tall lady appeared. Her long black dress had a white skeleton on it that glowed in the candlelight. She poured a jug of water into the bowl.

"I'm Jackie, Polly's mum," she said. "Have you ever tried apple bobbing, Ethan?"

He shook his head and stared at the skeleton.

"You lean over the bowl," said Polly, "then you pull out an apple by biting into it."

"But you can't use your hands," said Jackie.

Polly stood in front of the bowl. She lifted her cat mask and put her hands behind her back, then bent down to the water. Suddenly she bobbed up with an apple in her mouth.

"Bravo, bravo," said Jackie. She looked at the stopwatch in her hand. "Five seconds!"

Polly took the apple out of her mouth and put it back in the bowl. She pulled down her mask. "Your turn, Mum," she said.

Jackie gave Polly the stopwatch. She bent over the bowl and put her hands behind her back. Her long curly hair dangled in the water, but she didn't seem to mind. Her head moved from side to side as she tried to bite an apple, but missed. Then she got an apple between her teeth, but it fell back into the bowl with a splash.

Polly giggled. "Ten seconds!"

Ethan watched. He'd never seen a game like this before. He started to guess how many seconds it would take Jackie to get an apple. At last she stood up. Her hair dripped with water, but there was an apple in her mouth. She took it out of her mouth and laughed.

"Brilliant!" said Polly.

Jackie did a funny little dance, twisting her arms one way and her hips the other.

"One minute and twenty-five seconds," said Polly.

"Never, ever give up," said Jackie. She threw the apple to Polly and dried her face with a towel.

"Do you want a go, Ethan?" Polly said.

Ethan shook his head. He liked the strange apple-bobbing game, but he wasn't ready to join in.

"Maybe next time," said Jackie. "Who's for some Halloween food?"

It was like she could see right into his stomach.

Polly turned on a side lamp by the sofa and the room was a little lighter. "Sit down." She pulled out a chair for him at the big table and he sat.

Polly and Jackie went to the kitchen. They came back with plates piled high with food, jugs sloshing with coloured drink. It was a proper feast with lots of different dishes, not like Mum's meals. Ethan couldn't imagine Dad eating this food.

Jackie flopped into a chair. Polly sat beside him.

"Now Ethan," said Jackie, "vampire blood, or bug juice?"

He pointed to a tall jug of green liquid.

"Good choice." Jackie poured some into a glass. It tasted of lime and lemonade. There were jelly worms floating in it.

Polly helped herself to some vampire blood.

Ethan wasn't sure which food to try first.

"Have some bat wings," said Jackie, holding out a plate. Ethan took two.

"They're chicken wings, really," whispered Polly.

"These are witch fingers," said Jackie, "and these are mummy hot dogs."

Ethan bit into a witch finger. It was a strip of pizza with a red pepper for a nail.

"Make sure you leave room for dessert," said Polly as Ethan finished his second mummy hotdog.

Polly got up and went to the kitchen. She came back with a big pumpkin cake frosted in orange icing.

"I used liquorice for the eyes and mouth." Polly smiled.

Jackie cut Ethan a big slice and he bit into it. It tasted of cinnamon and orange; you could see the lumps of pumpkin.

Jackie stood up when they'd finished eating. She took a candle from the lounge sideboard and held it in front of her face so it shone with white light. "Time for our little Halloween ritual." Her eyes were wide. "We used to do it in the garden. From now on, we'll do it on the stern deck. Will you take my place, Ethan?"

Polly jumped up from her seat. "We'll go on to the stern deck and spin three times," she said. "We'll look into the water without blinking. That bit's new. Then we make a wish. You'll do that, won't you, Ethan? Better than trick or treat?"

Ethan frowned. He wanted to join Polly, but how could he make a wish?

"Ethan?" Polly looked so excited. She bent down to him and whispered, "It's OK – we wish silently, in our heads."

I can do that. He nodded.

"Come on, out you go." Jackie ushered him up from his seat. "Before you turn into a pumpkin."

The whole boat was lit by candles. Polly led him through the kitchen, past the bathroom and a door that said "Polly's Room". Then they were at the very back of the boat in a bedroom with a double bed and bright patterned bedspread.

"Mum's room," said Polly.

They climbed up the steps from Jackie's cabin and on to the stern. The deck was much bigger than *Deity's*. Ethan went to the horse-shaped railing and looked out at the midnight-blue water.

"Step back and reach out your arms to me," said Polly. Ethan's heart fluttered. He stepped back and did as she said. Polly stretched her arms towards him.

"Cross them like this." She crossed one wrist over the other. He copied her. She took his hands. Ethan's flushed hot. Her hands were warm. He hoped his were, too.

"Now we spin," said Polly.

She began turning, leaning back so their arms were a straight, strong line. Ethan began to turn too, and soon the lanterns were just a coloured blur.

Polly closed her eyes. "One."

It was exciting, spinning. Like being on the rope swing at his old tree house, when Dad used to push him and he soared into the sky. Then he felt it again, that same fuzzy feeling in his chest that he used to get on the swing.

I miss my tree house.

"Two," said Polly.

Why don't I go there any more?

They were spinning really fast now.

"Three."

Ethan counted in his head. Then Polly began to

slow and he felt disappointed.

Don't stop.

Ethan took smaller steps so he slowed. Polly let go of his hands. He was dizzy when they stopped; he stumbled a little and hoped Polly hadn't seen.

"Come over here, Ethan." Polly stood by the railing. "Look into the water and stare until you really have to blink."

He tried hard not to blink, but he couldn't stop thinking about the apple bobbing, the delicious feast and the spinning.

"You blinked." The voice came from behind him.

Ethan turned. Jackie stood at the top of her cabin steps. She held a big white cylinder. It looked a bit like a lampshade. It was hollow in the middle.

Polly turned to face them. "The paper wish lantern!"

"The last bit of the ritual," said Jackie.

"We light a lantern every year," said Polly.

Polly held one side of the lantern and Ethan held the other.

Jackie pulled out a lighter from her dress pocket and lit the lantern from underneath.

"Have you had fun?" Polly asked him.

Ethan nodded. If he could speak he'd tell her just how much.

"Close your eyes and make your wish, Ethan," said Polly. "Then we'll let the lantern go."

He held one side of the lantern and Polly held the other. Jackie took her hands away.

Polly shut her eyes.

Ethan shut his eyes, too.

I wish to speak again.

I wish I could speak.

"Have you made a wish?" asked Polly. Ethan opened his eyes and nodded.

"Me too," said Polly.

They took their hands away from the lantern. It rose up, filling the night with a yellow glow. He turned his chin to the sky, watching the lantern float higher and higher. They watched until they couldn't see it any more.

"That's what it's all about," said Polly. "Magic."

"Come in, Ethan," said Jackie. "Take some apples. Your mum can make a crumble."

Ethan left Polly gazing up at the sky. He followed Jackie through her cabin past the bathroom and

Polly's room and into the kitchen. He scooped up some apples from the bowl and put them in his fleece pockets. They made his trousers wet, but he didn't mind: he could stay on *Moon's End* for ever.

He glanced at the clock on the kitchen wall. It was wrong. It said seven p.m. His watch said one a.m.

"Time passes too quickly," said Jackie. "This clock slows down time."

Polly appeared at his side. "I'll see you out."

They climbed the bow stairs. The pumpkin's grin looked friendly now. Polly lifted its top and blew out the candle. Ethan could smell the smoke.

Polly pulled up her mask and it ruffled her hair. "I know what you wished for, Ethan," she said. Her green eyes sparkled in the darkness. "I wished it too."

CHAPTER

5

Ethan stepped off *Moon's End*'s plank and turned right down the towpath. He panicked until he found the torch and flicked the switch. The beam of light shone down on his trainers. He walked on, dancing the light along the bank so he didn't get too close to the water.

The stars looked brighter now, like Polly had dipped a pin in silver paint and touched them up for his walk home. The air was cold; it hadn't nibbled at his fingers when he was on *Moon's End*'s stern. Ethan zipped up his fleece so it covered his mouth. He remembered the wish.

Could I make it come true?

There was a stirring up ahead, the rustling of grass. He stopped. It must have been a hedgehog or badger. He waited to hear the noise again: silence. He turned back to *Moon's End* but her lanterns weren't lit any more. Slowly, he started to walk again.

Deity's bow was a couple of boat lengths away when Ethan saw a little orange light in the darkness, on the bank, near the stern. He drew a sharp breath. It was the glow from Dad's cigarette. What was Dad doing up? Did he know Ethan had sneaked out? If he knew, he'd be furious. Ethan turned off the torch. It might not be too late. Dad might not have seen the light from his torch. He could wait until Dad went inside, then creep past *Deity* to his cabin. That way, he wouldn't get into trouble.

"Who's there?"

The little glow tumbled to the ground. Dad had dropped his cigarette. Ethan thought about running and hiding by the hedge, but that might make a noise. It was better to stay still.

Dad turned on his lamp. It was too late to run: Ethan was caught in the lamplight.

"What are you doing out here?" Dad spoke louder

than normal as he came closer. "Where have you been?" He said each word like it was more important than the last.

Dad put his hands on Ethan's shoulders. He bent down so their eyes were level. Ethan could smell the smoke on Dad's lips. "Well?" he said.

Maybe if he told the truth, Dad wouldn't be so cross.

Ethan pointed at *Moon's End*.

"You went for a walk?"

He shook his head.

"You went to that boat?"

Ethan nodded.

"Come inside."

He climbed down the bow steps and into the lounge. Dad came in behind him. The wall lamp above the sofa bed went on. Mum sat up in bed, her eyes squinting. "What's going on? Ethan, why are you up?"

Because Polly invited me to her boat for Halloween.

"Jake, why's he up?"

"He's been to that new boat," said Dad angrily. "What's going on, Ethan?"

Mum got out of bed, her hair was loose around her shoulders. She tugged Ethan close and cupped his face in her hands.

"You don't go out at night-time." She was speaking fast, like the words could run away with her, like she might get angry too. "You don't go anywhere without telling us."

"Did they ask you there?" said Dad.

Ethan nodded, but he didn't want Polly or Jackie to get into trouble.

"Anyone could be prowling about. You've scared the life out of me, Ethan."

Ethan looked at Dad. He tried to say it with his eyes.

I'm sorry.

He reached into his pockets and put the apples on the sideboard.

"She's got a little girl," said Mum, "about his age. I've seen her on the bank. Is that who invited you, Ethan?"

"Well?" said Dad.

He nodded.

"I'll go down the canal," Dad said. "Find out what all this is about."

Ethan shivered and shook his head again and again.

"It's all right, Jacob. I'll go and meet them," whispered Mum. "I'll explain."

"No. Go to bed, Ethan," said Dad.

"What if he tells us where he's going?"

Please.

He wasn't going to bed yet. Not until he knew he could see Polly again. But Dad led him out of the lounge, through the engine room and into his cabin.

Dad let go of Ethan's arm. He looked down at Ethan. He sighed. "I wish you could *tell* me why you went." Dad shut the door.

Ethan sat on his bed. But he couldn't just climb in and go to sleep. He heard Dad shouting in the lounge and Mum telling Dad to calm down. What if he never saw Polly again? She wanted to help him.

Ethan switched on his little bedside lamp. His thoughts were all jumbled up. He needed to sort them out. He turned on his laptop and started to write. His page had become a squire now. He was learning to fight with a sword, but his stomach still somersaulted when he thought about going into battle one day.

Ethan saved his new entry and put the laptop on the floor. Dad was still shouting in the lounge. Ethan hated arguments. He hadn't meant to upset anyone. He wished he could to go back into the lounge and tell Dad why he'd gone to *Moon's End*.

He turned out the lamp and lay back on his bed. He imagined the wish lantern, rising up, filling his dark cabin with a yellow glow that made anything seem possible.

He had to see Polly again.

They had to make the wish come true.

CHAPTER
6

Ethan sat up in bed the next morning. A lovely smell filled the cabin. Mum always made bacon sandwiches when Dad was in a bad mood: it was his favourite breakfast.

Dad didn't have any gardening jobs. He'd be on *Deity* for most of the day. Ethan wouldn't be able to keep out of his way for long. What if Dad started shouting about last night? Ethan didn't know how to show him he was sorry.

Ethan drew back the curtain of his cabin window. He could see *Moon's End*'s blue stern, where he and

Polly had made their wish. The bacon smell was making his stomach ache with hunger now. He got up and washed and dressed. He touched the painted castle on his wardrobe door for good luck. He took a big breath and crossed his fingers behind his back as he walked out of the engine room and into the lounge.

Please let me see Polly again.

Dad was leaning against the countertop holding his coffee cup. Mum stood next to him. The air smelt bacony, but it still felt heavy.

"You're up," said Mum. She nodded to the sofa. "Come and sit down."

Mum sat next to him on the sofa.

Ethan took a breath.

Mum looked right at him. "Promise you'll never go off like last night again." The blue in her eyes looked brighter when she made him make a promise.

Ethan nodded.

Mum stroked his cheek and hugged him tight.

"I'm sorry I got angry last night," said Dad. He sipped his coffee. "I was worried about you being out by yourself."

Ethan smiled. Dad wasn't so cross with him any more.

"It's tough guessing what's inside that head of yours sometimes," Dad said quietly.

Ethan looked at the floor. Dad meant it was hard because he couldn't speak to him and Mum and tell them how he felt. Dad sounded upset because he wanted to understand but couldn't.

"Me and Dad have been talking," said Mum. "I went to see Polly's mum this morning. We've decided you can see Polly, but only in the daytime, and you still have to do all your schoolwork."

Ethan let out a big breath. He nodded quickly in case they changed their minds. Behind his back he uncrossed his fingers.

It worked.

"It's good you've made a friend," said Dad. "But we always need to know where you go and who you're with. You can't just sneak out without telling us."

Dad brought Ethan a bacon sandwich and Ethan grinned.

When Ethan had finished eating, Dad handed him a piece of paper. It said Gardening Services in big spidery letters. At the bottom was Dad's mobile number.

"Pin it on the noticeboard, will you, Ethan," Dad said.

The business must really be struggling. Dad never needed to advertise for work. Normally he just used word of mouth.

Ethan had to pass *Moon's End* to get to the noticeboard. He couldn't help staring at her stern, remembering the glow of the wish lantern.

Polly.

She was kneeling on the canal bank with her back to him. She had a paintbrush in her hand and there was a red paint pot on the grass.

He stood behind her and watched as she painted letters on the side of her boat.

THE CANAL

Polly turned around. "Ethan!" The tip of her brush made little circles in the air. "You came back. We're poem painting."

He smiled.

The pumpkin was gone from the end of *Moon's*

End's roof. Instead there was a red sign propped up by a flowerpot and facing the bank.

Hot Chocolate and Pancakes

Jackie stepped clumsily off the bow plank and on to the bank.

"We're painting poems on *Moon's End*'s blacking," she said with a wide grin. "If we like it, we'll keep it. If we get shy, we'll paint over it."

"I've got something for you, Ethan," said Polly. She handed Ethan her brush and headed to *Moon's End*'s bow.

"We didn't scare you off last night, then?" Jackie giggled.

Ethan shook his head.

Polly came back with a small blue rectangle in her hand. She held it out to him. It was a notebook. "You can write down what you're thinking," she said.

Ethan stared down at the notebook. He knew he should be pleased, but he wasn't. Even though he'd wished he could talk when he was on *Moon's End*, even though Polly said he should only *write* his words, he didn't know if he could share them with her. Mum was the only person who saw his writing. Dad had tried to get Ethan to use a notebook after he'd stopped speaking. But he couldn't use a notebook back then. It made him too nervous. He didn't know why.

"What would you like to write, Ethan?" asked Polly.

Not yet.

"I'll leave you to it," said Jackie. "Let me know if we get any customers." She climbed on to the stern and into her bedroom.

He looked up at Polly. Was she angry? She was trying to help, but he couldn't let her.

"It's OK, Ethan," whispered Polly. "You don't have to write anything if you don't want to."

Polly wasn't at all angry. Polly still wanted to be friends.

Ethan took the notebook. There was a little white pencil in the metal coil. He lifted the blue cover and saw an empty white page. He ran his finger over the smooth paper. It was perfect, like the rectangle of snow that had covered *Deity*'s roof last winter.

"It's OK." Polly smiled and her eyes shone.

"Keep it."

Ethan nodded. He ran his finger over the page once more. He slid the notebook in the pocket of his trousers to keep it safe. His fingers brushed Dad's notice and he took it out.

"Were you going somewhere?"

He pointed east down the canal. He showed Polly the advert.

"You're going to put it up. Shall I walk with you?"

He nodded. He liked listening to Polly's words tinkle up and down. She spoke a lot, but everything she said was interesting. Polly *liked* speaking.

Polly stayed close to him, her steps bouncy. They passed *Moon's End*'s bow.

"Does your dad need more work?" asked Polly.

Ethan nodded.

"Does he get cross sometimes because he's worried about it?"

Ethan nodded again.

"My dad needed work a while ago. He lost his job. He got cross. He found a new one. But it didn't make any difference. Mum still wanted to come away."

Merlin was hunting in the hedge. Ethan bent over to stroke her.

"Is she your cat?"

He nodded.

"Your boat cat," Polly said quietly. Polly picked up Merlin and she didn't wriggle. "It's not Mum's fault we left. Her and Dad were arguing a lot." She tickled Merlin under her chin and made her purr. "I had a cat at home, but we didn't bring her with us. It wouldn't have been fair." She leant her cheek against Merlin and stayed like that a while.

Then, gently, Polly put Merlin on the ground. They carried on walking down the canal.

"You're lucky to have three of you."

They stopped at the noticeboard. Ethan pinned up Dad's advert in the middle, so everyone would see it.

"Do you need to get back to *Deity* now?" said Polly.

Ethan nodded. They started walking.

"Maybe tomorrow you could show me more of the canal?"

He nodded again and again. He had that fuzzy feeling in his chest when he thought about spending more time with Polly. It was the same feeling he'd had on *Moon's End* at Halloween when they were spinning. Polly had made him remember how much fun it was soaring high in the tree-house swing. One day, he wanted to take Polly to the swing.

They reached *Moon's End*'s bow.

"I'm going to finish my poem now," said Polly. "Bye, Ethan. Keep the notebook safe."

Ethan touched his pocket and smiled.

CHAPTER 7

The next morning, Ethan sat on his cabin floor and wrote in his journal. The page had written Isabel a poem as a token of his affection. He hoped Isabel would help him feel brave enough to go into battle alongside his master so he could become a great knight, but he was worried she might leave the castle soon.

When he had finished writing his journal entry, Ethan took his notebook out of his pocket and stared down at the first page. Yesterday, Polly had asked what he wanted to write. Now there was a question he needed to ask her. He couldn't ask a question by nodding or shaking his head, or by shrugging his shoulders. He had to ask on paper. He had to stop the question swirling in his head and put it on the page.

Ethan took a big breath and slid his finger into the coil. The pencil popped out. He'd write the question now, when he was by himself. Then Polly wouldn't be watching him, waiting to see what he had to say.

Ethan touched the nib to the page and pressed down gently. He started to write. His hand shook. He'd keep his writing small to begin with so he wouldn't feel so nervous.

Ethan finished the last word. He shut the notebook and put it in the pocket of his jeans. He could show Polly his paper words, couldn't he? She'd shared the secret about her dad. She'd given him the chance to make his wish. And she'd wished for him to speak, too.

Ethan could go to *Moon's End* now. His lessons were finished for the afternoon, so he could explore the canal with Polly. Dad had gone to quote on a job. Mum was at the sink washing the lunch plates. She turned and smiled.

"Off to see your new friend, Polly?"

He nodded.

"Don't go too far down the canal."

Ethan stood on the bank and pressed his nose to *Moon's End*'s window. Polly was curled up tight on the lounge sofa, like a cat. She was reading. He gently knocked the glass with his knuckles.

Polly leapt up and waved. A few minutes later, she stepped off the bow plank in her red coat and green hat and scarf.

"Where are we going?" she asked.

Ethan nodded east and they started walking. He couldn't wait to show Polly all his favourite places.

"We're going exploring," said Polly, her eyes shining with excitement. "Are you keeping the notebook safe?"

He patted his pocket to tell her, but he didn't take it out.

"Good."

They passed the noticeboard. Ethan pointed to the white iron bridge that stretched over the water to the left side of the canal.

"Brilliant," said Polly. "I've not been on this side of the canal before."

They stopped in the middle of the bridge and looked down at the water, and the roofs of their boats. Then they jogged down the bridge steps. If they kept going for five more minutes, they would come to the wood.

"Ethan," said Polly, "do you ever get lonely?"

He shook his head. But then he thought about it. He hadn't felt lonely before Polly arrived. He'd had Mum and Dad. But now Polly was here and he liked having a friend to explore with.

"Was your mum always a boater?"

Not until she met Dad.

Deity had brought Mum and Dad together. One day, Mum had been sitting on the canal bank, painting *Deity*. Dad came off the boat to go to work. He said she made the canal look beautiful and that he worked with colour too, on his gardens. The next day Mum came back to the canal and gave Dad the picture of *Deity*. Then Mum started going to work with Dad so she could paint his gardens. And then they fell in love.

"Have they ever left the pound?" said Polly.

Ethan nodded.

They went to Thailand before he was born. They even took *Deity* off the pound and cruised the British canals one summer. Then Mum got pregnant with him and she had to leave art school. But Dad still said that one day, when the business was doing well, he'd rent an art studio in town, so Mum had space to paint on big canvases instead of tin jugs. And Dad wanted to take them all back to Thailand.

Ethan and Polly came to the hilly field and leant over the metal bar gate. There were cows snuffling their noses against the grass as they ate. Polly reached out and touched one cow's rubbery nose. It opened its mouth and licked her hand with its big tongue.

She giggled. "I've made another canal friend."

Ethan felt a rush of happiness. Polly had said they were friends out loud. Now he knew it for sure. He hadn't had a friend since he'd stopped speaking. He'd had two at school, when he used to speak, even though he spoke quietly and didn't say as much as the other boys. But then he stopped talking. And the older boys had started teasing him. And one day, Ben and Archie started playing with other boys in the playground instead of him. Sometimes Ben and Archie had joined in the teasing.

Polly was different. It didn't seem to matter that he couldn't speak; they could still share the canal and have fun together.

They kept walking past the stone tunnel, towards the edge of the wood.

"It's like a magic forest," said Polly, looking up at the criss-crossing branches.

She tapped Ethan on the back and ran off into the wood, her feet sending a flurry of leaves into the air.

"Ha!" She turning back, laughing. "You're it. Bet you can't catch me!"

Polly sped off and her scarf streamed out behind her. Ethan ran after her. He remembered this game. Catch. He'd played it at school. He was almost within arm's reach of Polly, but then she got even faster. She started darting left and right. She wove through the trees, circling one tree and then another. Ethan had to catch her. He ran faster. Soon he was closing in on Polly as she did a figure of eight around two trees. He stole her hat. She laughed.

"OK, my turn."

Ethan ran off into the trees. The wind whipped his face and the leaves crunched under his feet. He didn't want to stop. He kept going until he was deep into the wood, where the trees grew taller and closer.

When Ethan looked back, he couldn't see Polly. He was getting near the edge of the trees, by the stone stile. He stopped for a moment and scanned for a flash of red coat. Then suddenly he felt a pair of hands on his shoulders. He jumped.

"Got you!"

He turned round.

"I didn't mean to scare you," said Polly with a grin. "I ran around the outside of the wood as a surprise."

Ethan let out a big breath. Polly liked surprising people.

"I'm tired. Shall we have a rest?"

Ethan nodded and smiled.

They sat on the stone stile.

Polly reached in her pocket and brought out a slice of cake with orange frosting. She broke it in two and handed him half. "From Halloween," she smiled.

It tasted just like Ethan remembered.

Polly looked down at her cake, but she didn't bite in.

"I love the canal," she said, "but I miss my bedroom and my house and my dad."

Ethan finished the cake and wiped his hands on his jeans. He took out his notebook. He turned the cover. He held up his words so Polly would read them.

How long are you staying on the pound?

CHAPTER 8

Polly's eyes were wide. "You wrote me a note. You used it."

She was quiet for a while. "I don't know," she said at last. "*Moon's End* is our home now, but soon we'll move on to look for a permanent mooring."

Any day they might move on and never come back.

Ethan looked up at the criss-crossing branches.

"What schoolwork are you doing at the moment?" Polly spoke fast, like she didn't want to talk about herself any more. Ethan turned the page and rested the notebook in his hand. He tried to write quickly. He didn't want Polly to get bored waiting for him.

Knights
I'm writing a knight's journal

Polly's eyes sparkled. "Brilliant." She put her cake back in her pocket.

"I loved school," she said. "I had lots of friends. I liked circle time and gym club. We were learning about the Victorians, but then we moved."

"Ethan." Polly turned her head to him. Her words were just a whisper. "Did you ever speak?"

Ethan flinched. He looked at her for a while. He nodded.

"Why did you stop talking? Was it something to do with school?"

Ethan shook his head. He shrugged.

He didn't know why he stopped. Not for sure. All he knew was that he used to speak, but he stopped four years ago. That's what Mary said. One day he felt really sick when he thought about speaking; he was too scared to talk to Mum or Dad, or his teacher or his class. There was something stopping him, but he didn't know what it was.

"You don't have to tell me unless you want to," said Polly.

Ethan popped out the pencil. He turned the page and wrote.

> I don't know why I stopped.
> I can't remember.

Polly nodded. "Words are beautiful out loud," she said. "I won't ever try and make you talk if you don't want to. But if you did speak, I wouldn't laugh if your words came out wrong. I'd just be excited that you tried to talk."

Ethan nodded.

"Do you remember how it felt to speak?" she asked.

He shook his head. He was used to not talking now. If he thought about speaking his mouth felt heavy, like it was nailed shut. But he did want to find a way to talk to Polly.

"Do you miss school?"

Ethan shook his head and put his notebook away. He didn't want to think about school.

"Look!" said Polly, pointing at the stream to the right of the stile.

Ethan stood up and beckoned to Polly. They went over to the stream. He tucked his jeans inside his wellies. Polly did the same. They waded into the clear water and let it run over their feet. Polly stomped, splashing Ethan's jeans. Ethan stomped back and splashed Polly and she laughed. For a minute they both stomped together.

He and Mum had dropped sticks in the stream once. They had raced to the little white bridge downstream to see whose stick got there first. Now, he wanted to race Polly.

Ethan bent down to the side of the stream and found two sticks the same length. He gave one stick to Polly. He held up one finger, then two, then three, then he pretended to drop his stick in the water.

Polly nodded like she understood. "We drop our sticks in the water. Like in Pooh Sticks, except we don't drop our sticks off the bridge."

Ethan nodded. She took the red hairband out of her ponytail and wrapped it round her stick, so they knew which stick was hers. They each held their sticks over the water at arm's length.

"No cheating," said Polly. "After three."

Ethan held up one finger.

"One," said Polly.

He held up two fingers.

"Two."

Then three fingers.

"Three!" shouted Polly.

They dropped their sticks and watched as the water carried them slowly away. Ethan pointed to the little wooden bridge. They started to run.

"I want to win!" panted Polly as they ran.

Me too!

Then they were out of breath, leaning over the bridge, gasping, watching to see whose stick came out first.

"Come on, stick," said Polly, shaking her fist in the air.

Ethan hoped his stick hadn't got stuck on its journey.

"Yes!" Polly jumped up and down as her stick floated out a couple of inches from his. Ethan smiled. Polly looked so pleased that he didn't mind losing too much.

They watched as their sticks floated away. "Bye sticks," said Polly, waving. "Can we keep on exploring?" she asked.

Ethan nodded. He wasn't ready to go back to *Deity* yet, either. They followed the little path out of the wood and turned left, away from the canal to the playground. Dad had brought him here all the time when he was small.

Polly sat on one swing and Ethan took the other. They began to sway. Then Ethan pushed off from the ground. He leant back, stretching out his legs. Soon Ethan had a fuzzy glow in his chest that grew until it felt like a swallow was bursting out from his stomach and soaring up into the sky. Polly was swinging as high as him. Did she feel it too?

The tree-house swing was even better than the ones at the playground. You could swing higher and further, right out over the canal.

Polly began to slow.

"Let's try the merry-go-round," she said excitedly.

Ethan skidded to a stop then raced her to the merry-go-round.

"Will you push me?" asked Polly, climbing on.

Ethan grabbed hold of the metal bar at the side of

the merry-go-round. He pushed against it, walking faster and faster, until the merry-go-round was moving so quickly he had to jog to keep up with it.

"Jump on!" laughed Polly.

Ethan leapt on the wooden deck and held on tight to the metal bar. The playground was just a blur. It was like spinning on *Moon's End*'s deck at Halloween. Ethan remembered his wish.

I want to speak.

I have to make it come true.

The merry-go-round started to slow. They jumped off.

"I feel dizzy," giggled Polly.

Ethan smiled. He wanted to say, "Me too."

Ethan pointed to the gap in the hedge at the end of the playground. They should be getting back. He didn't want to make Mum and Dad worry. If they took the short cut through the hedge they could loop round and pick up the towpath a bit further down the canal. Then they could turn and head home the way they'd come.

They picked up the canal near the start of the railway tracks. The water looked different down here, yellowy green, like it was sick.

"I'd like go down there one day," said Polly, pointing further up the canal.

If they kept going that way they'd get to the tree house. Ethan wanted to show Polly that part of the canal, but now he was near, he felt nervous. He didn't know why. Maybe one day, he'd feel brave enough to take Polly there.

They turned away from the railway tracks and started walking home.

When they reached *Moon's End*, Polly lifted the paint pot and the brush from the bank.

"If you want to write a poem, there's lots of room. We'll paint over it after, if you don't want anyone to see."

Ethan looked at *Deity* and took a big breath. He took the brush and dipped it in the paint. He reached down to the blacking on the side of *Moon's End*. His brush began to paint letters. His letters made words. Polly didn't say anything; she just watched.

I WISHED TO SPEAK AGAIN
WILL YOU HELP ME?

Ethan stood up and turned to face Polly. He gave

her the brush. His heart raced with excitement.

"Yes," said Polly, her eyes shining. "You haven't lost your words, Ethan. They're fluttering round and round in your head all the time. And they come out when you write. Now you have to let them out into the world by speaking. Why can't you speak?" Polly put her hand on his sleeve. "What are you scared of?"

Ethan took out his notebook. He turned the page and wrote:

I don't know. But I don't want to be scared any more.
I want to find out why I stopped.

Polly hugged him quickly. "We'll find your voice," she whispered.

Everything was different with Polly. She didn't get upset or angry. She liked knowing about his voice. She wanted to help him. And she believed in magic.

Do you want to explore more tomorrow?

wrote Ethan.

Polly nodded hard. "I want to see everything," she said.

Ethan turned a page.

Meet me here at eight o'clock
tomorrow morning.

"Brilliant!" said Polly.

Tomorrow, he was going to show Polly the pond.

CHAPTER 9

Ethan couldn't sleep that night. He kept tossing and turning. He was thinking about the tree house. How he'd wanted to take Polly there, but he didn't feel ready. How scared he had felt being close to it, but how he didn't know why. When at last he fell asleep, he started to dream. He dreamt that Polly was standing next to him. They were underneath the tree house. They heard a *crack!* They looked up. There was a boy stamping on the floor of the tree house. He kicked the walls and shouted rude words. Then it was Dad who was standing next to Ethan, not Polly.

Dad was shouting at the boy, "Get down!" Dad's face was all scrunched up and pink and his eyes were burning with anger.

Ethan was a knight in his dream, but still he wasn't wearing any armour. He lifted his shield to his face so he couldn't see the boy. He wanted to escape on his horse, but it was nowhere to be seen. Then Dad vanished and when Ethan lowered his shield, the boy had vanished too.

The next morning, Ethan leapt out of bed and dressed quickly. He opened his wardrobe and took out his dipper net and bucket. He had to be fast. He had to stop thinking about the dream. It made his breaths come quick and stomach feel tight. Had something happened at the tree house?

There was a tap at Ethan's cabin window. It was eight a.m. Two green eyes peeped through the gap in the curtains. Ethan waved goodbye to Mum as she sat on the sofa eating breakfast. He grabbed a banana from the fruit bowl on the sideboard and climbed the bow stairs.

"A fishing net," Polly beamed as Ethan stepped off the bow plank and on to the towpath. "And a bucket.

We're going fishing?"

Ethan smiled. He handed Polly the dipper net. He pointed west down the canal, away from *Deity* and *Moon's End*. Once they reached the pond, the bad dream might stop swirling around his head.

"I've never fished before," said Polly. "Will you teach me?"

Ethan nodded. He'd show her how to dip the net in the water and scoop up a catch of little fish. He'd show her how good it was living on the canal and teach her new things, so she didn't miss home. Then maybe Polly would stay on the pound. Maybe Jackie could find a permanent mooring not too far from *Deity*.

They began walking. They passed the clearing where Dad kept the van. The van wasn't there because Dad had a job on this morning. Ethan felt the dream begin to swirl in his head. He turned to Polly, hoping she'd say something to make him forget it.

"I like being on the canal," said Polly. "I like being able to walk to *Deity* to call for you. I couldn't walk to my friend's houses at home; they lived too far away. My dad had to drive me." She sighed. "I spoke to Dad last night. He sounds really unhappy without us."

They turned away from the canal towards the wooden stile in the hedge.

Polly frowned. "Aren't we fishing in the canal?"

Ethan shook his head and smiled. He liked surprising Polly.

Polly swung her leg over the stile. Ethan held out his hand to steady her.

They started walking across the field.

"You're good at adventures and surprises, Ethan," smiled Polly.

Ethan felt a warm glow in his stomach. They could see the circle of reeds around the pond now. They went over the little bump in the field and looked down on the water.

Polly turned to him, her eyes wide. "I lived in the middle of a city before I came here. We didn't have ponds just down the road."

Ethan led Polly to his favourite spot at the edge of the pond, where the reeds weren't too thick. The water was green and murky, but clear enough to see the fish.

"Can I try?" asked Polly. "I want to try all by myself."

Ethan nodded. Polly held the net too high over the water. It was upright instead of on its side, ready to dip. But he'd let her have a go anyway.

"I can see some fish." Polly pointed at the water. There was a shoal of minnows darting towards them.

"Tell me when," said Polly.

Ethan nudged her gently with his elbow.

"Now?" She turned to him and he nodded.

Polly scooped the net into the water, but she was too slow and the minnows swam away from the net.

Polly lifted the empty net out of the water. "I missed," she said, frowning. "I'm going to try again."

She held the net over the water. They waited for another shoal. Ethan nudged Polly. Polly scooped, but she was too fast and the net made a splash, startling the fish, sending the shoal in different directions.

Polly stamped on the ground. "Rubbish."

Ethan had never seen Polly cross before. It was funny. He grinned.

"Don't laugh. I'm just not very good at fishing," she shrugged.

Normally, Polly was good at everything. Ethan liked her even more now. Because it meant she was like him – good at some things, but not as good at others. And she got cross, just like he did sometimes. But Ethan didn't want Polly to be disappointed because she hadn't caught anything.

Ethan took hold of the net by the handle, just above Polly's hands. He helped Polly inch it out over the water and then twist the stick so the net was on its side. He waited for the minnows to swim towards the net, then together, they scooped into the water.

"We got one," said Polly as they lifted out the net. "Maybe next time I'll catch my own fish," she said as they watched the fish wriggle.

Ethan dipped the net in the water so the minnow could swim away. Then he scooped the net along the bottom of the pond to see what else he might catch.

"What's that little spotted-lizard thing?" asked Polly as he lifted out the net and let it rest gently on the grass.

Ethan took out his notebook. He could teach Polly about pond life.

Newt,

he wrote.

A smooth newt.

"Hello, little newt," said Polly, kneeling down next to the net. "And that?" she said, pointing to a brown insect with long back legs.

Waterboatman.

"It's shaped like a little rowing boat," said Polly.

Ethan held the net in the water so the newt and the waterboatman could swim away. He picked up a small, flat stone from the side of the pond. He wanted to show Polly how to skim stones.

Ethan bent down low to the ground. He held the stone between his thumb and first finger, to keep it flat. He brought his hand towards his chest like he was sowing a handful of seeds, and then he swung it back out towards the water, hard.

The stone spun through the air, getting closer and closer to the water. But it didn't sink; instead it skimmed over the water's surface, bouncing on it, one, two, three, four times.

Four. It was his new record.

"Magic!" said Polly. "Can I have a go?"

Ethan handed Polly a stone. She held it between

her thumb and finger. She bent low. She spun it over the pond just like he had. Polly watched excitedly as the stone bounced once, then twice.

Ethan clapped.

"Not bad for my first time," Polly beamed.

Ethan clapped again. Then he dipped the net in the water, lifting it out fast, and swung it towards Polly.

The water splashed Polly and she giggled.

"Ethan!" she laughed. "Ethan!"

Ethan laughed too. He had taught Polly to skim stones and made her laugh. She'd stopped worrying about her dad and he hadn't thought about his dream for ages either.

Ethan dipped the net in the water and splashed Polly again. She scooped up some water in the bucket and threw it at him. Soon, it was a water fight. It didn't matter that the water was cold and smelt funny or that it made Ethan's coat wet.

"Stop, stop," said Polly at last. "Let's play a game. We played it at school once. I'll lead you back to the stile, but you keep your eyes closed. I'll be your guide. You mustn't open your eyes till I say. I'll make sure you don't walk into anything."

Ethan nodded and shut his eyes. Polly took his arm and they started to walk up the hill away from the pond.

It was strange walking with your eyes shut, not knowing how near the stile you were. But after a few footsteps it didn't feel so scary. Ethan worried that he might trip over or walk into a tree, but he tried to concentrate on the feel of his boots brushing the long grass and the cold air tingling his cheeks.

"You can stop now," Polly said, much sooner than he'd expected.

Ethan stopped.

"Open your eyes," said Polly.

They were standing by the wooden stile.

"We did it," said Polly with a big grin.

CHAPTER 10

They walked back to *Deity*.

Polly pointed to the dinghy that was tied to *Deity's* stern. "Could we use your dinghy one day?" she asked excitedly, and Ethan nodded.

Mum climbed out of the bow doors and waved. She came to join them on the towpath. She smiled and said, "Hello, Polly, lovely to meet you."

Polly smiled back and her cheeks went pink.

Ethan felt for his notebook.

Can Polly stay for dinner?

Mum read the note and beamed. She put her arm round Ethan. She was pleased he was using the notebook, he could tell.

"Would you like to have dinner with us, Polly?" Mum asked. "We're having sausage and mash and I've made apple crumble with the apples you gave us."

Polly nodded. "I'll just go and tell my mum."

Ethan watched Polly run off down the canal. He put the dipper net and bucket on top of the boat. He followed Mum down the bow stairs and into the lounge. Dad was taking the crumble out of the oven and the sweet smell of baked apples filled the whole boat.

"I hear we've got a special guest for tea," said Dad, and Ethan smiled. "I'll be on my best behaviour."

Ethan helped Mum lay the table. When there was a knock on the bow doors, he climbed the steps and led Polly down into *Deity*.

"So, Polly," said Mum when they sat down for tea. "How are you finding life on the water?"

"Fun," said Polly, in between a mouthful of sausage. "Ethan's been showing me the canal."

"Nice boat you've got," said Dad.

"It's lovely," said Polly. "But I prefer this one. It's more homely."

Dad smiled. "Is it just you and your mum?" he asked.

Polly nodded. She looked down at her food. Ethan knew Polly felt bad because her dad wasn't with them.

"Are you not at school at the moment?" asked Mum.

"I will be," said Polly. "When we move and find a mooring to settle on."

"If you'd like to borrow some schoolbooks, let me know," smiled Mum.

"And if your mum needs a hand with the boat, just give me a shout," said Dad.

"Thank you," Polly smiled.

"Let's try that crumble," said Mum.

"Can I see your cabin, Ethan?" asked Polly when they'd finished eating.

Ethan led her into the engine room and opened the door to his cabin.

"Wow," said Polly. She ran her fingers over the wooden walls. "It's so snug in here." She frowned.

"Where's your bed?"

Ethan undid the latch on the tall cupboard and his bed unfolded.

"Magic!" said Polly. She turned to the corner of the cabin. "You've got your own little stove." She touched the white painted castle on his wardrobe. "And a storybook castle."

Ethan nodded and pulled out his secret drawer. Polly's Halloween note was rolled up inside.

"My note," said Polly. She looked up at the ceiling. "My cabin isn't as fun as yours. There isn't a hole in the roof. I don't have a fold-down bed, or a castle, or a stove. I'd rather sleep in your cabin."

Ethan stretched out his duvet and they sat on the bed.

"Your mum and dad are nice," said Polly softly. There were tears in her eyes. "I wonder what my dad had for tea."

She was quiet for a while. She looked down at the duvet. "Sometimes I wonder really bad things," she said. "I lie in bed and I can't sleep. I wonder what if Dad thinks we don't care and he moves house and I can't find him. Or what if he meets another lady with a daughter and she moves into my bedroom and my dad prefers her to me?"

Polly looked up at him, her eyes glistening. "Do you ever wonder scary things, Ethan?"

He nodded hard. He'd thought he was the only person who wondered things like that. If he could speak, he'd tell Polly all the things he wondered about. What if Dad had to drive lorries? What if he was made to go to school? What if something bad happened to Mum or Dad? What if Merlin went missing and never came back?

"How do *you* stop wondering?" asked Polly, her eyes fixed on his.

Ethan thought for a moment.

He got his notebook from his pocket.

> I take a big breath,

he wrote.

> To make me brave.
> Then I let it out really slowly.

"OK," said Polly. "I'll give that a try." She took a big slow breath and let it out with a funny sigh.

"There," she said.

Polly started laughing and Ethan laughed too. Then they heard a meow. Merlin padded into the cabin and jumped on the bed, as if she didn't want to miss out on the fun.

Polly stroked Merlin. "Ethan, have you tried to talk since you stopped?"

Ethan shook his head.

"They were mean to you at school, weren't they? Was it because you didn't speak?"

He nodded.

Mum and Dad want me to go back he wrote.
To another school.

"Maybe you should," said Polly. "Your mum and dad would love that. And they'd love it if you spoke." Polly was quiet for a moment. "My dad would love it if I went back home."

Polly looked like she might really cry this time. He wrote fast:

You can borrow Merlin for a night. So you don't get lonely.

So you don't miss your dad as much.

Polly scooped up Merlin and held her tight. "Can I really?" she smiled.

Ethan nodded. Polly looked happier now and it was all because of his idea.

"Amazing," said Polly. She stood up with Merlin in her arms.

"Can you show me more of the canal tomorrow?" she asked.

Come over tomorrow morning at ten.

Polly nodded hard. Ethan stood up. He led Polly back through the engine room and into the lounge.

"I'm borrowing Merlin, is that OK?" said Polly to Mum and Dad, who were sitting on the sofa.

Dad laughed. "Of course you can, Polly," said Mum.

"Brilliant," said Polly. "She's going to sleep in my cabin. I'll bring her back in the morning."

"Walk Polly home, Ethan," said Dad.

"And take some crumble for your mum," said Mum, handing Polly a plastic container. "Come and see us anytime," she said. "It's great that Ethan's found a friend on the canal."

That night, Ethan woke with a jump. He was hot all over. He'd had the tree house nightmare again. But this time it was more real, more frightening. He and Dad were underneath the tree house. The boy was stamping on the tree-house floor, kicking the walls and shouting rude words. But he was laughing cruelly this time, twisting his face into frightening shapes and shaking his fist at them. Planks were falling from the floor of the tree house. The boy ripped off a plank from the roof and threw it to the ground. The noise stabbed right through Ethan and made him flinch. And Dad was even angrier than before. Dad was shouting, "Stop!" so loudly it hurt Ethan's ears.

Ethan turned on his lamp. Why wouldn't the nightmare go away? He hated having it, but he couldn't stop it.

He had to go back to the tree house and find out what had gone on there.

Mum and Dad would be at work tomorrow.

Tomorrow, he'd take Polly to the tree house.

CHAPTER 11

Ethan gazed out over *Deity's* bow, down the misty-morning canal to *Moon's End*. Where was Polly? To get to the tree house they had to go far down the canal, further than the railway tracks. But he had to do it.

The bow deck was cold under his bare feet. He shivered. A pair of moorhens bobbed past *Moon's End* and into the mist. He'd got up early to do the work Mum had left for him. She was setting up the market stall this morning and Dad had a little landscaping job in town. They'd driven off in the van, but in two hours Dad would be back. Ethan wasn't allowed in the dinghy by himself, but it was the only way to get to the tree house and back in time.

Dad had taken two weeks to build the tree house. It had been Ethan's seventh birthday present. That day, Dad had tied a scarf over Ethan's eyes. They paddled down the canal for what felt like for ever. "Look," said Dad as he had lifted off the blindfold. And there it had been.

The tree house was on No Man's Land. No Man's Land was a strip of grass beside the canal that didn't belong to anyone. Dad used to row Ethan there every Saturday, past where the train tracks curved away from the water. They'd tie the dinghy to the big tree, unwind the rope ladder and climb up to the tree house.

Dad would hold the ladder as Ethan climbed. They'd sit on the wooden floor of the tree house and dangle their legs over the side. They'd eat their picnic, looking down at the murky green water and the tourist boats chugging past.

There was nothing to get in the way up there. None of Mum's boxes to load on the van. No boat chores. Dad would give him the oars on the way back so Ethan could learn how to row. Ethan couldn't remember the last time they'd been to the tree house. Why had they stopped going there?

Polly was coming down the canal. She was carrying Merlin. She wore her coat with the hood up. She stopped next to the bow plank.

"I can't wait," she said. A swirl of mist came out of her mouth.

She stepped on to the plank. It wobbled like always, but she didn't slow down. She put Merlin on the deck. "I gave her some chicken for breakfast," she grinned.

Ethan took out the notebook and pencil from the back pocket of his cords. He drew a dinghy, a matchstick boy paddling, a matchstick girl sitting behind.

"We're taking the dinghy?" Polly's eyes were dancing.

Ethan nodded. They walked down the bow plank and on to the bank. They went to *Deity*'s stern and Ethan started to undo the rope that tied the dinghy to a metal ring.

"Where are we going?" asked Polly.

Under the white bridge. Through the stone tunnel. Past the train tracks. To where the ducks are bigger. To my old tree house.

Ethan climbed into the dinghy. He coiled the rope at his feet and picked up the oars. Polly climbed in next to him.

Ethan began to row, past *Deity's* stern and east down the canal.

"A proper adventure," said Polly, her eyes wide. "This is like something out of a storybook. Are you allowed to use the dinghy on your own?"

Ethan shot Polly a look and she knew right away what he meant.

"It's OK," she said. "I won't tell anyone."

They passed *Moon's End* and went under the white bridge. His words weren't on the blacking any longer. Polly had painted over them.

Drops of water fell on them in the long dark tunnel. They came out into the gloomy light, surging towards the railway tracks. There were no boats to pass down here, no fishermen or walkers. The air smelt like Ethan's jumpers when they'd been hung inside the boat to dry.

It was further than he'd remembered. They'd been gone twenty minutes. They'd passed the wood and the stone steps that led up to the lane, the overgrown banks and the trees that leant into the water, but they hadn't even reached the railway line. Ethan felt nervous as they reached the weeping willow tree, but he didn't know why. It was like something bad had happened under it.

"Ethan, what's that?" Polly grabbed his oar and drew a sharp breath.

He looked over the left side of the dinghy. A brown lump floated in the water about two metres away. He rowed closer. The lump rolled over. Ethan flinched.

It was a dead dog.

"What happened to it?" asked Polly.

Ethan stopped rowing. He should turn around and row back. They should never have come this far. What if the dead dog was a warning? What if something bad was waiting for them at the tree house? What if there was a horrible boy kicking the tree-house walls and yelling rude words, just like in his nightmare?

"Is it much further?" asked Polly.

Ethan shook his head. He took a big breath. If he didn't see the tree house in real life, he might never find out what his nightmare meant. He started to row. He had to reach the tree house. He needed to find out what had happened.

CHAPTER 12

Ethan rowed hard. The railway tracks were curving away from the canal now: it was the beginning of No Man's Land. The dead dog was behind them, but there was still a knot in Ethan's stomach. They were just a metre from the tree house now. He rowed left, out from the middle of the canal to the big tree. The dinghy was touching the bank when Ethan stopped rowing. He gripped the oars tight.

Polly scrabbled out of the dinghy and on to No Man's Land. There were clumps of brambles and tall stinging nettles under the big tree, but she weaved around them and gazed up at the huge branches.

Ethan climbed out of the dinghy. He lifted out the rope and stepped around the nettles. He tied the rope to the tree trunk, just like Dad used to.

"This was your tree house, wasn't it?" Polly asked.

Ethan nodded.

The tree house looked just like it had in the nightmare. It was falling apart. Bare branches cradled the wooden shell of the house. Planks were missing from the floor, and only half the roof was left, but it was still there, and the swing still hung from the branches.

There was a sign on the ground, in the tall grass. The wood was splitting down the middle, but you could still read it. Ethan picked it up.

ETHAN'S HOUSE

"Your sign," said Polly.

Polly sat on the swing and held the ropes. She lifted her feet from the long grass and he pushed her gently, just how Dad had pushed him.

"Again!" Polly dropped her head back and her laugh spiralled up through the branches. "Higher!"

He kept pushing. Polly swung out over the canal and back to the tree. Her plait came undone and her hair fell in front of her eyes, but she didn't seem to mind as she soared out over the canal. Then she was back under the tree, twisting the ropes from side to side, putting her feet on the ground.

Polly climbed off. "Your turn," she said.

Ethan put the sign on the ground and grabbed the swaying log seat. He sat and lifted his feet. Polly pushed him and he was moving, swinging forward, then back. There was a flicker in his heart. She pushed him a little harder. The flicker grew stronger until he had that glow in his chest. Ethan soared out over water's edge and back to Polly. Out again, then back.

He put his feet down and stood up.

Polly tipped back her head. "Let's go up."

Ethan shook his head. It looked like someone had wrecked it. It didn't look safe. And he didn't feel safe standing next to it either. He wasn't sure if something bad had happened in the tree house, but it felt like something could.

Polly was already climbing up the tree trunk. The rope ladder had gone, but she didn't need it.

Ethan clapped his hands and stamped his feet. He kicked the trunk to try and tell her.

No! Come down.

But Polly was already at the top, lifting herself on to the wooden floor. Ethan stepped back from the tree so she would see him.

"Come up!" she said, looking down on him.

He kept clapping, stamping his feet.

"What's wrong, Ethan?"

And then he remembered.

He heard Dad from a long time ago, from their last visit to the tree house, shouting, "Get down!" It wasn't inside a dream any longer. Ethan could remember what had actually happened back then, in real life.

Ethan looked back up at the tree house. Polly wasn't there any more. Instead there was a big boy with ginger hair and a crooked nose, a boy in a blue coat and white trainers, kicking at the walls and shouting out bad words. It was the boy from his dream. And Dad was on the ground next to Ethan, his head dropped back, his face red, yelling at the boy to stop. "Stop! Stop! Stop!" And Ethan had shouted "Stop!" too.

Ethan blinked. Polly was in the tree house again. He heard a crack. One of the planks fell to the ground. Then a flash of red was falling through the air: Polly had slipped. She screamed as she hit the ground. She was lying on her side. He rushed to her.

Ethan felt dizzy, like his whole body was swaying. Polly moved her arm. Slowly she got to her feet. She brushed the dirt and leaves off her red coat.

"It's OK," she said. "I was silly. Lucky I wasn't too high up."

Ethan went over to Polly. He wasn't cross with her now he could see she was safe. He'd remembered the tree house getting wrecked. He and Dad had caught the boy wrecking it the last time they rowed here. That was what his dream had been about.

Ethan took out his notebook and wrote Polly a note. His hand shook.

He held out the pad.

Something bad happened here.
The last time I was here with Dad.
We found it being wrecked.
I've had nightmares about it.

Polly fixed him with her green cat eyes.

"Were you still speaking then?"

Ethan nodded.

"Maybe that's why you stopped," she whispered.

Ethan paddled fast. Dad would be home in thirty minutes; they had to get back to tie up the dinghy.

It was raining hard by the time they reached the railway line. They put up their hoods. Water trickled off Polly's hair and down her coat. Ethan tucked the tree-house sign inside his coat.

He checked his watch at the white bridge. Dad would be home in twenty minutes. Ethan's arms ached, but there wasn't time to rest.

Ethan used the same knot as Dad to tie up the dinghy. Polly climbed out and on to *Deity's* stern and Ethan followed. A drop of water flicked off Polly's hair on to Ethan's face as she turned back to face him.

"Whatever happened at the tree house, it's important," she said. "You have to try to remember more. It might help you to speak again."

Ethan nodded. Polly was right. He felt it inside of

him. Small and hard like a pebble.

"I'd better go," said Polly. She looked at him but her eyes didn't sparkle. She was quiet for a moment. Ethan knew her head was heavy with thinking. That there were words she wanted to say, but that it would hurt her inside when she said them.

"I spoke to my dad yesterday," she said at last.

She didn't look at Ethan; instead she wrapped her arms tightly around her chest and stared down at the stern deck, and Ethan wanted to hug her.

"I was right," said Polly quietly. "He's so unhappy."

Ethan wished he could say something really kind to make it all better. He felt a rush of anger.

It's not fair.

He thought fast for an idea to cheer her up. He reached into his pocket and brought out the notebook.

Come fishing on the pond.
You can catch your own fish.

Polly smiled and nodded.

"Come to *Moon's End* first," she said. "For hot chocolate. At nine in the morning. Then you can tell me exactly what happened at the tree house."

Ethan nodded. He watched Polly climb off the plank and head back to *Moon's End*.

Back in his cabin, he pulled off his trainers and stripped off his clothes. He found a dry pair of trousers and a jumper.

Heavy footsteps fell on the bow stairs. It was Dad: he called out, "Ethan?"

Ethan sat on his cabin floor. He turned on his laptop to write in his journal. "All right?" Dad hovered at Ethan's door.

Ethan looked up.

Dad held open the door. His fingernails were black with soil. Dad's fringe was the same brown as the reeds on the canal bank, just like his. Ethan wanted to nod but his stomach felt heavy; he didn't know why. He'd felt just the same when Polly stood up in the tree house.

"Ethan? Do you need a hand?"

He remembered the big boy in the blue coat and Dad yelling, "Get down!" He wanted to write a note to Dad about the nightmare, but he didn't know where to begin. Dad would be furious that he'd gone out in the dinghy all by himself. And he was

116

too afraid of what Dad might tell him about the tree house.

Dad's eyes looked empty and tired. "I'll just leave you to it," he said.

Ethan nodded. Dad closed the door. He turned off his laptop. He didn't feel like writing his journal.

CHAPTER 13

Ethan took his dipper net and bucket from the bow-side roof. He'd write Polly a note about the tree-house boy while they had hot chocolate. He would tell her everything he had remembered. Then they could go to the pond. If he and Polly were really lucky they might see a dragonfly sitting on the reeds, shining blue and green in the sunshine.

Ethan stepped down off the bow plank and on to the towpath. He walked quickly; he had to meet Polly.

"Ethan!" called Dad.

Dad was behind him on the towpath. He was loading up his tool bag ready for work.

He turned to Dad and held up his net. *I'm off to the pond.*

"I need your help," said Dad.

Ethan pointed down the canal to Polly. He didn't want to go with Dad. He could see Polly waiting outside *Moon's End*. She was smiling and waving. He waved back.

"It's all right, I'll talk to her, son." Dad headed down the canal to *Moon's End*. Polly walked along the bank to meet Dad. Dad spoke to Polly and Polly nodded.

"Off we go," said Dad when he got back. "Polly's not upset. She can join us another day. I thought we'd spend some time just the two of us."

Ethan leant the dipper net against the side of *Deity*. He looked back at Polly and she waved again. Dad started walking down the canal path to the clearing where the van was parked and Ethan followed.

They climbed in. Dad turned the key and the van lurched up the lane. At the crossroads, he didn't turn left to town like Mum always did. He turned right. Soon they were twisting through tiny lanes. There weren't any houses or buildings, just flat fields with spindly hedges. Dad nodded to the bag of liquorice allsorts on the dashboard, but he didn't say where they were going or what kind of job it was. Dad's overall smelt earthy. That was how he had always smelt, even when Ethan was little.

They turned up a long track with tall trees on either side. The van juddered over the gravel, then stopped outside a big grey house.

"Out you get," said Dad, nodding to the door.

It looked like a gardener hadn't visited the house in years. The grass on the lawn was up to Ethan's knees. It was good that Dad had got this job, but it would take him a long time by himself.

Ethan followed Dad to the back of the van. "Take this," Dad said.

The tool bag was heavy. Dad took a shovel and a bag of peat from the van. "This way," he said.

They walked away from the house to a row of flower beds. They didn't have any flowers, just a few shrivelled-up shrubs. "Here we are." Dad pointed to a circle-shaped flower bed.

Ethan dropped the tool bag on the ground. Dad dropped the bag of peat and lifted his shovel and sliced into the earth. Then he started digging, churning up the soil with the sharp blade.

Little lumps of earth flew up and landed at Ethan's feet. He kicked at them with the toe of his trainer. What was Polly doing now?

Dad stopped digging and turned around.

"Have you got the flask, Ethan?"

Ethan bent down and looked in the tool bag. He shook his head.

Dad laid his shovel on the ground. He came over and searched the bag. "For God's sake!" Dad kicked the bag of peat. Thud: the sound echoed in Ethan's chest. In a second, he wasn't in the tatty garden. He was standing on the canal bank near the train tracks. Dad was facing the big boy with the blue coat and ginger hair. Then the big boy was stumbling back, falling on to the towpath by the weeping willow. His head fell on the concrete last. Thud.

Had Dad hit the boy? Hit him so hard that he fell and knocked his head? Was that the bit of the memory Ethan had forgotten? It couldn't be. Could it? It didn't make sense. There must be another explanation. Another reason why the boy fell. But he'd remembered Dad being angry with the boy. He remembered him falling back.

"Ethan?"

Then he and Dad were back at the tatty garden with the empty flower beds.

Dad sighed. "*I* forgot it. I'm sorry. It was *my* fault, son," he said.

Dad was quiet for a while. He didn't pick up the shovel. Instead he reached into his pocket and held out a little blue rectangle.

"I found it yesterday in the lounge. I'm glad you're using it."

It was Ethan's notebook. It was open at his message to Polly.

I don't know why I stopped.
I can't remember.

Dad passed Ethan the notebook.

"You don't know why you stopped speaking, do you?" Dad said quietly, his eyes glistening.

Ethan looked past the flower beds to the spindly trees in the distance. His breath felt tight; Dad never spoke much about his voice. Not these days. He used to talk about it all the time.

"Ethan?"

He looked at Dad and shook his head. Dad let out a big breath. "Didn't think so. Sometimes it's best not to remember, Ethan. Sometimes it's best to leave the past behind."

Dad stepped towards him and laid a hand on his shoulder. Ethan began to feel dizzy. He and Dad weren't in the garden now; they were back near the tree house and the vandal boy was lying under the weeping willow not moving and Dad was looking down on Ethan, with his hands on Ethan's shoulders and his face all pink, his eyes wide with fear.

"Go! Run home." That's what Dad had told him to do that day.

Then Ethan was back in the overgrown garden and there wasn't a boy on the ground and when he looked up Dad's eyes weren't full of fear, just grey and empty, but Ethan still felt dizzy.

Dad took his hand off Ethan's shoulder. He crouched down and looked at him. "You've got to be careful in life, Ethan," he said. "Can't let the past take over, like weeds in a flower bed."

Ethan nodded and tried to listen to Dad.

"If you come out with me at weekends, I'll train you up."

Dad stood up. He opened the bag of peat and lifted a stack of flowerpots from the tool bag. He reached into the pocket of his overall and brought out a packet of seeds. He lined the pots up in a neat row. Ethan watched him.

Dad put a handful of peat into each flowerpot and sprinkled in some seeds. He filled the pots with more peat. He bent over them and pressed down on them gently with his fingers. "Here, you have a go."

Ethan knelt down next to a flowerpot. He started to squash the peaty soil. He didn't like the way it stuck to his fingertips, how it got under his fingernails and made them black. He tried to press down hard just like Dad, but his hands were shaky.

He tried to think of all the good things Dad did for him, like singing him to sleep while playing his guitar, Dad's voice slow and soft and beautiful. Or making little wooden narrowboats that he could float on the canal. But he still couldn't forget that boy, falling back with a thud, lying out on the concrete.

Why didn't Dad want him to remember?

CHAPTER 14

Dad didn't say much as they loaded the van that evening. They drove away from the big house. They parked the van in the clearing; the clock above the steering wheel said it was almost six. Dad undid his seat belt. Ethan got out. He wanted to run down the canal to *Moon's End*, to write down everything Dad had said and show it to Polly. But there wasn't time.

Ethan left half his shepherd's pie at dinner.

"Not hungry?" Mum's forehead crinkled up. She looked at him with narrow eyes. She reached across the fold-out table and took his plate.

"You should be after all that work," said Dad.

"You look tired, Ethan," said Mum. "I think you need an early night."

Ethan didn't shake his head. He wanted to go to his cabin. His whole body was heavy from carrying Dad's tools and the bag of peat. He didn't feel like sitting on the sofa with Mum and Dad.

Ethan pushed back his chair. He padded out of the lounge, through the engine room and into his cabin. He turned the latch at the top of his bed cupboard and the mattress and quilt unfolded. He tugged the quilt over his shoulders. The cabin was freezing cold, too cold to sleep. Even the little corner stove wasn't warming it. Frosty air crept in through the little hole in the ceiling and wriggled into his bed. It nibbled the bit of bare skin between the top of his pyjamas and the bottom of his T-shirt. His feet were as cold as the water in the canal.

Ethan grabbed both sides of the quilt and pulled it tightly under him. Now he had a cocoon, like a caterpillar, to keep out the cold. He went over Dad's words at the big house, again and again.

Sometimes it's best not to remember, Ethan.

Sometimes it's best to leave the past behind.

He went over the words so many times that they got jumbled up in his head.

Best not to remember sometimes.

His head was tired, heavy; he was falling asleep.

He dreamed about himself and Dad, sitting in the dinghy, rowing home from the tree house. A big boy with ginger hair stood on the towpath ahead, facing them, looking out over the water. The dinghy heaved through the water faster than ever before. Dad reached out with his oar and pulled them close to the bank. Dad climbed out of the boat and on to the grass. He said "Stay there," but Ethan didn't want to. Dad went over to the boy. Dad's mouth was opening wide; he was shouting at the boy. But Dad's words were silent. They didn't make a sound.

Ethan scrabbled on to the bank. There was a thud. The boy was falling back, back, back on to the concrete. Thud. The big boy was lying there with blood on his face . . . the big boy wasn't even moving. . .

Ethan woke with a jump. He sat up and grabbed a handful of quilt. He wasn't in the little boat any longer. He was in his bed. His back was sweaty and he'd wriggled out of his cocoon. The clock on the wall said five past midnight. He turned on his lamp. It was OK. There was no ginger-haired boy lying there, in his cabin. His room looked the same as always.

Ethan lay back. He curled up in a tight ball like Merlin. What if the boy was dead? What if Dad had hurt him?

He shut his eyes. He was back at *Deity* after Dad said, "Run home." Mum was on the sofa, sleeping. He stood watching, wanting to wake her and tell her about Dad and the boy. But his arm wouldn't move because he was afraid to say the words out loud, and Dad always said "Don't Get Mum Upset" because there was a baby called Maisie in her tummy that had tried to be born early. And when Dad got back that night he didn't tell Ethan what had happened, he just came into his cabin and said, "Let's not tell Mum about that boy". And Ethan didn't speak again after what he'd seen. And he didn't speak the next day either. He felt too sick. And if he did speak, he might tell someone and Dad might get in trouble.

Dad didn't talk about the boy again. And then Maisie was born too early and she died. Mum was always crying, and when Ethan tried to think about why he'd stopped speaking, his head was foggy.

Ethan opened his eyes. He had to tell Polly what he had remembered.

Sometimes it's best not to remember, Ethan. Sometimes it's best to leave the past behind. That's what Dad had told him, and now Ethan knew why.

Dad didn't want him going off at night, but everything in Ethan's head was all mixed up like muddy water and the water wouldn't clear. He had to make sense of his memories. Ethan put on his fleece and pulled his cords over his pyjama bottoms. He found his trainers on the floor. He took his torch from the hook beside his bed and turned it on. He climbed the cabin stairs and stepped out on to the stern deck.

The frosty grass crunched as he ran. There wasn't time to look up at the stars tonight. He had to get to Polly.

He was out of breath by the time he got to *Moon's End*. He knocked on Polly's window that overlooked the bank and he waited, but she didn't pull back the curtain. What if Polly didn't wake up? He'd have to turn around and go back to his cabin, but he wouldn't be able to sleep, he'd just lie there remembering the nightmare. He knocked again, harder this time, and the glass hurt his knuckles. A light went on. The curtain pulled back and Polly's white face looked out. She opened her window.

"Ethan, what is it?" she said. "What's wrong?"

He pointed to *Moon's End*'s bow.

"I'll let you in."

Polly was wearing white pyjamas. He followed her through the lounge and the kitchen and into her cabin opposite the bathroom. On her bed was a quilt with coloured butterflies, but he was too dizzy to notice the rest of the room.

Polly reached over and touched his cold hand.

He pulled out his notebook and told her.

> I had to help Dad today.
> Sorry.

"Don't worry. Are you OK?"

> I remembered.

"Remembered what happened at the tree house?"

He nodded.

"And why you stopped speaking?"

Ethan shrugged. He didn't know for certain.

Maybe.

"Sit down," she said gently.

Ethan sat on her butterfly bed.

"It's OK," Polly said. "Take your time. You don't have to tell me until you're ready." Ethan nodded. He looked down at his notebook. He was scared, but he had to tell Polly. He couldn't keep it to himself any longer.

He wrote one word on each line: the words might not look so horrible if he wrote each one alone.

I
Think
Dad
might
have
hurt
a
boy

He looked up at Polly. She just looked back at him; she didn't say anything. He needed her to say something. He wrote again. In sentences this time, so she could see it properly. See how terrible it might be.

I think Dad might have hurt the boy who wrecked the tree house. The boy fell and couldn't move.

Polly looked down at the words.

"Are you sure?" she said at last. "But he's your dad. He loves you. I know he gets a bit cross, but do you think he'd do that?"

Ethan didn't want to think it could be true. But his brain kept swirling with memories: the boy's face all scrunched up as he staggered back. Dad's eyes swimming with panic. How still and white the boy's face was as Dad said, "Run home."

Why couldn't Ethan remember what had happened before that?

"You don't know exactly what happened, do you?" said Polly.

Ethan shook his head.

"*We* have to find out," said Polly. She didn't look afraid. "We have to find out exactly what happened, *tomorrow*."

He nodded, but he didn't understand what Polly meant. How could they find out?

"We have to go to the library," she said. "They'll have old newspapers from years back. We can look through them. I did it for a school project once."

Ethan was scared of looking for the truth. But he didn't feel quite so dizzy now that he'd told Polly.

He turned to a new page.

Can I sleep here tonight?

Polly nodded. She took a pillow and some cushions from her bed. She lay the cushions on the floor, and then she lifted her butterfly quilt and spread it over them. Polly had made him a bed.

Ethan knelt on the cushions and climbed under the quilt.

Polly opened a cupboard and brought out a blanket. She got into her bed and turned out the bedside lamp.

"Go to sleep," she whispered.

CHAPTER 15

"Ethan, wake up. You've got to get home."

Where was he? Ethan sat up slowly. He saw the flower-shaped clock on the wall. Polly was kneeling on the floor next to him. He remembered running down the towpath to *Moon's End*. He remembered about Dad and the boy.

It was six. If he left now, he'd get back to his cabin before Mum and Dad woke up. They would never know he'd stayed at Polly's.

Ethan pulled back the quilt and stood up.

"Here." Polly passed him his trainers. "We have

to get to the library. Is your mum going to town today?"

He tried to remember what day it was: Saturday. Dad was walking to a job nearby, so he didn't need the van. Mum had to go food shopping.

Ethan nodded.

"I'll come to *Deity* at nine-thirty."

He turned back before opening Polly's cabin door.

"Maybe it's a good thing that you're remembering, Ethan," said Polly.

He didn't understand what Polly meant: the memories made him feel like his head was full of silt. The silt wouldn't settle. His head wouldn't clear.

"Maybe if we find out what really happened, we can get your voice back."

Outside, the sun shone on the frosty ground. Slowly, Ethan walked to *Deity*. In just a few hours they would be at the library. Today, he might find out the truth about why he had stopped talking.

Ethan hurried along the canal bank, past the lounge to the back of the boat. Once inside his cabin, he took off his outside clothes and kept on his pyjamas. He got back in bed to warm up. Dad would be leaving for work in half an hour; then Mum would get up and Ethan could write her a note. He reached for the laptop and turned it on. He started to write his journal.

His page was worried about his father. He'd dreamt his father was wanted by the sheriff. But he didn't think his father could have done anything wrong. Could he? He had to leave the castle to find out the truth. He had to prove his father's innocence.

Ethan heard Dad shut the bow doors as he left for work. Ethan got up and turned a page in his notebook. His hand shook as he wrote out the question in the engine room. His legs felt weak when he got to the kitchen.

He stood at the sink next to Mum and held out the notebook.

Take me and Polly to the library?

Mum smiled.
"Of course," she said.

CHAPTER 16

The van swung into the marketplace and stopped. Mum turned to him.

"I'll pick you up from here." She looked at her watch and smiled. "At half past eleven, OK?"

Ethan nodded. His hands were sweaty. He'd lied to Mum. He'd written in another note that they were going to the library to get knight books. Now he wished that was true.

Polly opened the door and climbed out. She didn't seem as nervous as he was. She had chatted to his mum the whole way there.

"Out you get, Ethan," said Mum.

He slid along the front seat and stepped out. He shut the door. The van moved away, juddering over the cobblestones.

"Where's the library?" asked Polly. "We've only got a couple of hours."

Ethan pointed to the high street. They walked quickly, across the marketplace to the charity shops and cafes. Ethan pointed to a little road off the high street. They turned into it. The library was just a boat length ahead – it was a little white building with a green door. Today he felt sick as he walked towards it. They stopped when they reached the entrance. Ethan looked at Polly. He took a big breath and led her inside.

The library was quiet, but it didn't feel peaceful. The silence seemed to fill every corner and hang off every shelf.

Ethan looked at Polly. "Over here," she said, and pointed to a metal staircase at the back of the room. Next to the stairs was a sign with an arrow: **Public Records**. Ethan had never been up there before.

They climbed the staircase. There weren't rows of storybooks, just lines of grey cabinets. The air smelt musty, like Dad's coat when it needed a wash.

A grey-haired man sat at a desk. "Do you need any help?" he asked.

"We're looking for the old newspapers," said Polly. "Copies of the local paper."

"Old newspapers," said the man. "Sounds to me like you're after the microfilm machine."

Polly nodded. "We're researching a school project," she said quickly.

The man got up from his chair. "What year did you want?"

Polly looked at Ethan. He held up four fingers. "Four years ago," she said.

The man walked over to a row of cabinets. He tapped the top of a cabinet with his fingers and it made a tinny noise. The man pointed to the top drawer.

"Here we are. Do you know the exact date of the newspaper?"

"We'll just look through the boxes, if that's all right," said Polly.

The man smiled. "When you've found your reel let me know. I'll show you the machine."

The man turned and went back to his desk.

Ethan reached out and grabbed the drawer handle. The drawer slid open and he remembered Dad's words.

Sometimes it's best not to remember, Ethan.

"Do you know which month it was?" asked Polly. He shook his head. His heart thudded. The drawer was stacked with rows of black boxes as big as his hand. Each box had a label with months written on it.

"What about the time of year? Spring, summer. . ."

White sun shining through cold air; a layer of papery leaves on the towpath.

"Autumn?" said Polly.

Ethan tapped Polly's arm. He nodded.

Polly lifted out a black box and put it on top of the cabinet. The label said:

September

October

November

Ethan turned to the man at the desk and held up his hand. The man came over to them.

"We're ready now," said Polly, picking up the box.

The man led them to an ugly machine perched

on a table. It looked a bit like a television. It had a big white screen that stared down at them. Below the screen was a metal spoke. In the middle was a small square of glass, like the lens on the toy microscope Mum bought him ages ago.

Polly put the box on the table.

"Take a seat." The man pointed to two orange chairs under the desk.

Ethan wanted to stand so that he was taller than the machine, bigger than the horrible news story they might find about a boy getting hurt on the canal. But Polly sat down, so Ethan sat too. The plastic chair dug into his back.

"Now," said the man, "do you know how to load the reel?"

Polly nodded. She flipped open the lid and lifted out a reel, slotting it on to the metal spoke. She unravelled the end of the film and stretched it across to the empty reel. She flicked a switch and the machine began to hum.

"That's right," said the man. "It's the blue button to look through slowly, the red one to look through quickly."

"Thank you," said Polly. "We'll be fine now."

Polly hovered her finger over the slow button. They waited until the man was out of sight.

"Are you ready?" she asked.

Ethan shook his head. He put his hand on top of Polly's.

"Do you want to do it?" she asked.

He nodded. He needed to know the truth.

Polly moved her hand. Ethan pressed down on the button. Pages of the *Herald* began to move across the screen: September stories. He could read the words easily. Safe stories mostly, about fêtes, football results or new car parks; adverts for pets and jobs and furniture. But sometimes they saw a story that made his stomach pull tight. Horrible stories about car crashes and fights in pubs – but nothing about a boy getting hurt on the canal.

Had he imagined it all? Had it just been a dream?

The machine stopped humming. The screen went blank. Ethan took his finger off the button. They'd looked through all the September newspapers.

Polly lifted the reel off the spoke; she dropped it back in the box and loaded October.

"We need to go faster," she said. "We haven't got long."

Ethan pressed Fast. More stories sailed past: New Nightclub, Council Job Cuts. The stories weren't too scary this month.

The screen went blank. It was the end of the October stories. Ethan took his hand off the button.

Polly put October back in the box and brought out a new reel. "November," she said. She put it on the spoke and stretched the film on to the empty reel. It was the last of the autumn stories.

Ethan pressed the Fast button. More stories flashed past. Suddenly, Polly pulled his hand off the button. The machine had stopped on a story.

Polly whispered. "That's the one."

He didn't want to read the big words at the top of the page, but he made himself look.

CHAPTER 17

Tuesday 27th November
Boy Dies on Canal Path

Polly grabbed Ethan's wrist.

"It wasn't your dad's fault the boy got hurt. Look!"
She pointed to the little words below the title.

Ethan started to read.

A sixteen-year-old diabetic who collapsed and
died as he walked along the Linford canal path
yesterday lost his life due to natural causes.

An inquest found that Steven Lucas suffered a
severe diabetic attack.

"The boy was ill," said Polly.

Dad didn't hurt the boy; the newspaper story
proved it. He knew Dad wouldn't do that. His dad
loved him.

Polly scrolled across the page to a photo. She
pointed. "That's him."

Ethan's stomach somersaulted. The boy on the
screen had a chubby round face; a straight nose. He
shook his head.

"It's not him, is it?" said Polly with a sigh.

They'd searched through the whole of autumn
now. They still hadn't found a story about his boy.
What did that mean? If his dad hadn't done anything
wrong, why had Ethan stopped talking?

He wanted to run out of the library, past the
cabinets, past the librarian, down the stairs and out
through the door. But they were in town and he
didn't know where to go.

Polly looked at her watch. She put the reel back
in the box and closed the lid. She pushed back her
chair and stood up.

"We'd better meet your mum," she said. "We're late."

Ethan couldn't get up. Nothing had changed. The memories still didn't make sense. He hadn't found out what had really happened. He reached into his pocket for the notebook and put it on the desk. He wrote big letters that took up the whole page.

WHAT NOW?

"I don't know," said Polly, tugging bits of fluff from her scarf.

She took the box back to the cabinet, and then she beckoned Ethan. He walked over to her, his trainers scuffing the carpet. They passed the man's empty desk. They climbed down the stairs. They left the books and the coloured cushions and walked out of the green door on to the street.

Mum was parked in the marketplace waiting for them. Ethan opened the van door and got in next to her.

"Didn't you get any more knight books?" asked Mum.

They were all on loan," said Polly quickly.

Mum parked the van in the clearing. She climbed out, and they got out too. Mum started walking to the towpath. Dad would be home for lunch now. Ethan would have to try and sit next to Dad and eat his lunch like nothing was wrong, even though his head swirled with questions. Ethan started to walk.

"Wait, Ethan," said Polly. "We could tell your mum about the nightmare."

He couldn't tell Mum. Talking about the tree house would remind Mum of Maisie, because Dad had built it just before she was born, so that Ethan wouldn't feel left out. Mum might get upset and not stop crying like before. And anyway, Mum would ask Dad about what happened at the tree house. What if Dad had hurt that boy? Dad might get taken away from him and Mum. Or Ethan might get taken from them. And what if Mum had kept it a secret? She might get in trouble as well.

"What about my mum?" asked Polly.

He shook his head quickly. No.

He took out his notebook.

I'm going to come up with a plan.

Promise not to tell anyone about anything.

"But this is bigger than you and me."

He wrote again.

PROMISE.

Polly looked at him. "I promise," she said. "You'd better go. I'll come to *Deity* this evening."

He ran to catch up with Mum as she reached the bow. They could go in together. That way Dad might not see he was upset. He wouldn't ask what was wrong.

"Go ahead," said Mum. "I'm popping down the canal to talk to a lady about the stall."

Ethan didn't move.

Mum smiled. "You'll be bored. Help Dad with lunch. I won't be long."

She began to walk. He felt sick as he watched her go. Just before she reached *Moon's End*, Mum turned back. She pointed to *Deity*. Ethan had to go inside.

There was only one thing he could do. He had to write Dad a note asking him what had happened.

The bow plank wobbled when he stood on it. He stepped down on to the deck of the bow; the little doors were wide open. He crouched at the entrance. His heart pounded but his feet kept moving. He was on the top stair, then the second and the third.

Dad was at the kitchen sink. He looked up and smiled. You could see the squiggles on his arm that meant "husband" in Thai.

"Been to town?" Dad dropped a plate on the pile with a clank.

Ethan took a big breath and let it out slowly. Dad looked at Ethan carefully. "Ethan?"

He couldn't keep it inside any longer: he had to know the truth.

Ethan reached into his pocket for his notebook. His hands shook more than ever as he pulled it out. The letters were shaky when he wrote.

What happened that day at the tree house?

He walked closer. He held the notebook high. The tears pricked his eyes.

Don't let it be true that Dad hurt that boy.

Dad looked at the note and squinted. He spoke slowly.

"What happened . . . that day . . . at the tree house." Dad sighed. "Sorry, I don't know what you mean, son."

Ethan turned the page. He didn't have armour like a knight to make him brave, but he'd keep writing. Dad's eyes were on him, crinkly around the corners and kind.

Ethan wrote bigger this time.

The boy who got hurt at the tree
house.
I remember him.

Dad frowned. "What do you mean?"

Ethan had to write one last note. He didn't know if he could do it. He turned the page and pressed down hard with the pencil so the words couldn't escape. The tears jabbed at his eyes like needles now.

DID YOU HURT HIM?

He held up the words. Dad looked at them. Ethan wanted to scribble them out, but it was too late now.

Dad didn't speak. He looked at Ethan, then he stared back down at the page.

Ethan pulled the notebook away.

"For God's sake Ethan!" Dad's face screwed up as he stepped towards him. But Ethan's feet wouldn't stay put. He bumped into the sink and a stack of plates crashed to the floor. Mum's best plates, but he had to run.

His fastest run ever, up the bow stairs. . .

"Wait!"

. . .on to the bow deck, along the plank and up the towpath. He didn't look back.

He'd run to *Moon's End*. He could stay on *Moon's End* for ever.

Ethan's stomach stabbed with panic when he reached *Moon's End*. The hot chocolate and pancake sign wasn't on the roof. He peered through the lounge window and through Polly's window, but there was no sign of Polly or Jackie. He climbed on to the bow plank. He tried the bow doors but they were locked. Where were they? Had they left the canal?

The fear stirred Ethan's stomach. He couldn't

go back to *Deity*. Not now. He didn't want to hear the truth. He wished he'd never asked Dad about the boy. He loved Dad. He could get by without his voice. He wished he hadn't started looking for it.

He started running again, his feet pounding the concrete towpath. He would run and run, past the tree house and away from the canal. Hot tears trickled down his face as he passed the white bridge. He would have to leave Mum and Dad. He didn't know where he would go, but what choice did he have? Ethan's chest heaved and his feet thudded the ground. Then he heard another sound: a thud, thud, thud that was out of time with his feet. It was coming from behind; someone was running after him.

Ethan looked back. He took a breath of cold air. Dad was at the bridge, his face all pink and his mouth wide open, gasping for air as he ran. Dad was just a boat length behind. Ethan was afraid of what Dad had to say.

"Ethan!"

Ethan kept running. He was nearly at the tunnel. A sharp pain snaked up his side. His feet pounded the ground as he made it past.

Thud, thud, thud.

Dad was still following him.

The pain cut deeper. Ethan was struggling to breathe, he was slowing down, his trainers were dragging on the concrete. Then he was bent over, fighting to get his breath. Dad was getting nearer. The grass and the water blurred. Ethan couldn't run, his body wouldn't let him.

Then Dad stood right behind him, panting loudly.

"What's . . . going . . . on? You . . . think . . . I . . . *hurt* . . . that boy at the tree house?"

The words swirled with the water and the grass. Ethan had seen the boy lying there, not moving; he'd remembered it. Hadn't he?

"I . . . didn't even . . . touch . . . him."

Dad was getting his breath back; each time he spoke he was angrier.

"He was . . . drunk, fell, hit his head."

It could have been an accident. But what if it wasn't? What if Dad had to hide it so the police never found out? So he didn't get taken away from them?

"He hit me. I asked him why he wrecked your tree

house. He decked me. He tried again and fell. Hit his head on the towpath. He was out cold, bleeding."

Ethan took a big breath and turned to face him.

"Who d'you think I am?"

But what had happened next? Dad had told him to run home when the boy was lying there and Ethan ran; he had left Dad with the boy. Ethan grabbed his notebook from his pocket. He turned a new page. He wrote fast.

Why did you make me run home?

He pointed at the page. Dad stepped towards him and read it. Then there was the crunching of leaves: someone was walking towards them. Ethan looked back. Mum. He'd forgotten all about her. She waved. "Hello, what're you two up to?"

Mum didn't know about any of this. But Ethan couldn't stop now. He turned the page. He wrote fast.

You never told me what happened to the boy.

Mum was just a few steps away. He held up the

notebook. Dad took it and looked at the page. Ethan reached out and took it back.

"What's wrong, Ethan?" Mum looked over Ethan's shoulder as he wrote again.

You told me not to tell!

Mum frowned. "What boy?" She looked at Dad. "What does he mean?"

Ethan's face went hot. The water and the grass blurred again. Did Mum know anything about it?

"That lad," Dad said. "Years ago, the lad that fell on the towpath."

Mum nodded like she knew all about it, like it wasn't a horrible secret at all. Ethan's head whirled with questions.

"He thought I hurt him," said Dad. "Thought it was all *my* fault."

"No, Ethan!" said Mum, her eyes wide. "It wasn't your dad's fault at all. Tell him!"

"I sent you home so you'd be safe," said Dad.

"It was an accident," Mum said. "The boy hit Dad, then fell badly. Cracked his head. He'd been drinking. Your dad called an ambulance. He waited with the boy till it arrived. They took him to hospital. He got better." Mum crouched in front of Ethan. "The police asked Dad if he wanted to press charges. He said no."

The boy hit Dad, but Dad stopped the boy getting into trouble for it. That was what Mum said.

"I thought he'd forgotten." Dad said.

Ethan tugged the loose end of wool on his sleeve. The stitches unravelled into a hole.

Mum took Ethan's hand. "We need to go home. We need to go home and talk about this."

They walked to *Deity*, the three of them in a row. Dad was next to him by the water. Mum was next to Ethan by the hedge. They passed *Moon's End*. He didn't know what he'd do if Polly had gone.

Dad pointed to the sofa when they got back. "Sit down, Ethan," he said.

Ethan sat. Dad sat next to him and leant in close. Mum stood watching.

"It wasn't my fault." Dad put a hand on Ethan's shoulder. "Do you understand, Ethan?"

The thud, the boy lying there bleeding. Ethan must have missed the middle bit when he was scrabbling up the bank. The truth bit – that the boy had tried to hit Dad, then tried again, but fell. Dad hadn't been trying to stop him remembering at the big house. Maybe Dad didn't know why he stopped speaking after all. Maybe Dad and Mum thought it was because of Maisie. Maybe Dad didn't want him to remember how unhappy they'd all been.

Dad's eyes drilled into his. They were glistening with tears. Dad was waiting for him to nod, to let him know it was OK now.

"Ethan?"

Ethan nodded again and again. Dad let out a big sigh. "Thank God," he said, looking up at Mum. Then Mum sat on the sofa too and Dad wrapped his arms around both of them and squeezed them tight.

That evening Ethan open his laptop and wrote a new journal entry. His page was reunited with his father and the truth was revealed. His father had not done anything wrong and he was no longer wanted by the sheriff. He would not go to jail. The page was relieved. He had known deep down that his father was a good man.

CHAPTER 18

Ethan sat up in bed and looked out of his window. It was a clear sunny day, a perfect day. He had to go to the pond. He got dressed and took his notebook from the chair. He wrote a note for Mum and Dad and left it next to the kitchen kettle so they wouldn't worry. The dipper net was still leaning against *Deity*. He took it up the towpath, over the stile to the pond. He found a spot at the side of the water where the ground wasn't too muddy.

Ethan watched a shoal of darting minnows. He bent forward and gently lowered the net. He tilted it ready to scoop. Out the corner of his eye by the stile, there was a flash of red. He looked up.

"Ethan!"

It was a red coat.

Ethan drew a sharp breath. Polly was back.

He stepped away from the water. He waved to her. His feet wouldn't stay still; he was jumping up and down and waving at the same time. Polly was running to him.

"Ethan!" Her plait was swinging. "Ethan!"

He started to run to her. The ground was soft and lumpy, but he didn't care if he fell. It seemed to take for ever to reach her. Her cheeks were pink. "We went into town yesterday. I'm sorry I wasn't around. Your mum said you got upset."

He wanted to tell Polly that he had missed her, even though she hadn't been gone very long. He could tell her everything Mum and Dad had said. Tell her Mum and Dad had explained all about the boy, that it wasn't Dad's fault, just like he'd hoped.

He brought out the notebook. He wrote it as quickly as he could.

The boy hit Dad.

Then the boy fell over and hurt his head.
Dad saved him.
Dad didn't hit him.
The boy was OK.

He held up the notebook. Polly finished reading. Then Polly reached into her pocket. "I went back to the library this morning." She held out her hand – there was a piece of folded paper in it. "Open it."

It was a tiny newspaper story, just a few lines of words.

Good Samaritan Saves Drunk Attacker

A drunken youth who vandalized a young boy's tree house and then attacked the boy's father owes his life to his victim. According to witness Tim Winger, Jake Meaden called Dominic Grey an ambulance and stayed with Grey after he fell and hit his head on the towpath while trying to assault Meaden. Grey suffered head injuries but is making a stable recovery at Linford Hospital. Meaden does not wish to press charges.

"I went back to the library yesterday to make sure we hadn't missed anything. I found this and photocopied it. It was only small. We must have scanned past it the first time around."

Ethan put his net on the grass behind them. Warmth flowed down his arms, into the tips of his fingers. The sunlight caught the water and dazzled his eyes. His chest felt fuzzy, like it had when he had been spinning with Polly or swinging out over the water at the tree house.

He held the story tight between his thumb and finger. He read it again. His dad was a hero and Ethan was so proud.

Polly touched his arm. "It's amazing, isn't it?"

He nodded and blinked back tears. He read it again. He shut the article in his notepad and carefully put it in his pocket.

"You can't have many pages left now," said Polly.

Eleven. Each time he used one he felt sad, even though he could get another notepad.

Polly bent down and picked up the net. She stepped so close to Ethan that their coats were touching.

"I'm going to catch a fish," she said.

Polly held the net on its side, just above the water.

A little shoal of minnows swam towards it. Polly scooped the net into the water, then lifted it above the surface.

Two little fish lay on the netting, tails flapping, glistening.

"I did it!" said Polly. She did the same little dance as Jackie on Halloween, twisting her arms one way and her hips the other. "See? Never ever give up."

He smiled. They watched them for a while, Polly's fish.

Then Polly lowered the net towards the water. "I don't want to keep them away from the others," she said. Polly dipped the net in the pond and the minnows swam free.

"You have to tell your dad you believe him," said Polly. "You have to tell him today."

Ethan nodded. Polly was right.

Can we go now?

he wrote.

When they got back to the canal, Dad's van was parked in the clearing.

"Do you want me to come in with you?" asked Polly.

Ethan shook his head. He wrote Polly a note.

Thank you, but I have to do it by
myself.

Polly hugged him tight. "Good luck, Ethan," she
said.

Ethan climbed down the steps and into the
lounge. Dad was on the sofa playing his guitar. Mum
wasn't around. Ethan went over to the sofa. "What
is it, son?" said Dad quietly, putting down his guitar.
Ethan took the newspaper story out of his pocket
and held it out.

"What's this?" Dad unfolded the piece of paper. He
stared at the headline.

"You found it," Dad said at last.

Ethan held out his notebook. Dad took it. His eyes
scanned across the words on the page and he read
them out.

You were a hero.

Dad smiled; his eyes glistened. He ruffled Ethan's
hair. "Thank you, son," he said. Then, slowly, tears
rolled down Dad's face and on to his jumper. Dad was

crying. Dad wiped the tears with his hand and Ethan sat down next to him. He turned a page. He wrote the words bigger than ever. He held out the notebook.

I'M SORRY.
I GOT CONFUSED.

Dad cried harder then. "I'm sorry too, Ethan," he said. "Sorry we didn't talk about that boy at the time." Dad pulled Ethan on to the sofa and hugged him tight.

"I love you, son," he said.

CHAPTER 19

Dad came into Ethan's cabin the next morning. "Up you get. I've got something to show you," he said.

They took the van and drove east down the canal, but Dad didn't say where they were going. They parked in the little lane that led to No Man's Land. Ethan followed Dad up the path towards the canal. That's when Ethan knew. Dad was taking him back. Back to the tree house. And his heart began to race with excitement.

Ethan didn't notice at first, not till they went around the side of the tree house to the front. Then the trees and the leaves seemed to swirl around him, but in a nice magical way, not a scary, bad-dream way, because the tree house had been mended. There weren't any planks missing from the floor. The roof was complete again now.

"What do you think?" asked Dad, grinning proudly.

Ethan smiled his big smile. He couldn't stop staring up at the tree house. It looked strong, sturdy, like it could survive anything. It didn't matter that the wood was a patchwork of different colours. Dad must have worked on it between jobs over the last couple of days.

Dad nodded to the ladder. "Let's go up."

As Ethan climbed, Dad held the ladder, even though it wasn't shaking. They sat on the floor and dangled their legs over the side. Ethan's chest felt fuzzy, even more than before, when they used to visit the tree house. As if he was swinging in the highest swing in the world, like a hundred swallows were bursting out of his chest.

Dad took two pieces of chocolate cake from his pocket. He gave a piece to Ethan; then he unscrewed the flask and poured.

"Here," he said. Ethan sipped. It was hot chocolate. Dad must have made it especially for him.

Dad was quiet as they looked out over the fields and the lanes, to their end of the pound. Then he reached into his bag and brought out the mended tree-house sign.

"Mum found the sign," he said. "You came back here."

Ethan nodded. Dad wasn't cross that he'd come all the way here by himself.

Dad brought out a hammer and a nail. He held the sign against the outside of the tree house and hammered it in place.

ETHAN'S HOUSE

"You must have missed coming here," he said.

Ethan nodded.

Dad turned to him. "Is that why you stopped talking?" Dad spoke quietly, like the words might cut his mouth. "Because you thought I hurt that boy?"

Ethan looked at Dad. He didn't nod. He didn't want to upset him. But Dad knew it anyway.

"I guess it must have been," Dad said softly. "We couldn't work out why. We wondered if it was because of Maisie. We took you to get help, but you didn't want to talk."

Ethan thought back to the nice lady. The games and songs she tried to play to get him to speak. But he hadn't been able to. He must have blocked Dad and the boy out on purpose, because he was so scared of what he'd seen. He must have been too scared to speak in case he told anyone and got Dad in trouble.

"We can get help again if you want to. It might be easier to sort out now."

Ethan nodded.

Dad put his arm around Ethan's shoulder and hugged him close.

Ethan could feel the tears pressing against the back of his eyes, trying to escape. He could hear Dad's heart beating and feel his warm breath on his neck.

Him and Dad back at the tree house.

Ethan's shoulders shook as he started to cry. Happy tears.

Then the tears overflowed, down his face, and on

to Dad's coat. And Dad hugged him and hugged him and didn't let go.

CHAPTER 20

I showed Dad I'm proud of him,

wrote Ethan.

I wrote him a note and showed him
his newspaper story.
And he's fixed my tree house.

"That's brilliant, Ethan." Polly didn't smile. She
hadn't smiled since she'd come to his cabin that
morning. It was as if she was sitting ten boat lengths

away, not right next to Ethan on his bed.

"Well done," she said.

She turned around and touched the white painted castle.

"Mum spoke to me about Dad this morning. She knows I miss him. They want to try to be together again. We're going to go home tomorrow, Ethan."

A shiver shot down Ethan's back. He felt sick, even though he always knew that, one day, Polly would move on. He imagined what his page would be thinking now. He would want Isabel to be happy, even though he was sad she was leaving. And he would hope that one day he might still become a knight.

Ethan felt for his notebook. It took him a while to write the words.

I don't want you to go.
I'll miss you so much.
But I want you to be
with your dad too.

"Thank you," said Polly.

Ethan put his arms around Polly and hugged her

tight. He didn't want to take his arms away. Polly was smiling when he let go, but there was a tear sliding over her freckles. "I'll miss you too," she said softly.

Ethan went into the kitchen and wrote Mum a note.

Will you take me and Polly to the tree house?

"Out you get," said Mum when they reached the little lane. "I'll pick you up in an hour."

"It's amazing," said Polly as they gazed up at the tree house.

Ethan started to climb the wooden ladder and Polly followed.

"I can see *Deity* and *Moon's End*," said Polly as they sat in the tree house.

Ethan was looking down on everywhere he'd been with Polly. The wood, the stream, the playground, the pond in the far distance. It felt good seeing it from high up, like getting a big hug.

"You can go further than the canal, Ethan," said Polly, kicking her legs.

What did Polly mean? The canal was home. He didn't need to go any further, did he? He could go to the library or the market now and again. And he could come here now, too.

"The canal's beautiful. You don't have to leave it completely. I mean, you're bigger than just the canal."

Ethan didn't understand, but it sounded important. He kicked his legs and breathed in the damp air, but he still didn't know what Polly meant.

"You could go back to another school and be happy. I know it." .

That night, they made up the air bed on the floor of Ethan's cabin, so Polly could sleep over.

Ethan opened his wardrobe and took out the model of *Deity* that Dad had helped him make.

"It's beautiful, Ethan, thank you," said Polly, running her fingers along the side of the model. She reached into her patchwork bag and brought out a book. "This is for you. It's my favourite book. *Charlotte's Web*. It's about a pig and a spider who become friends. The spider helps the pig by spinning special messages in her webs. It's a sad story because the spider has to leave the pig, but it has a happy ending."

Thank you,

Ethan wrote.

His notebook was full now. But he could get a new notebook.

That night, after they got into bed, Polly read to Ethan from *Charlotte's Web*. She did a low, kind voice for Charlotte the spider, and a high, squeaky voice for Wilbur the pig.

Ethan lay there listening to Polly read. It made him wonder if he would ever speak again. But slowly, he stopped wondering about his voice, and he just listened, and before long he was inside the story with Wilbur and Charlotte and her special messages. And slowly, Polly's words lapped over Ethan and gently swept him to sleep.

CHAPTER 21

Jackie was on the bank untying the bow line when Ethan and Polly got to *Moon's End* the next morning. The hot chocolate and pancakes sign wasn't on the roof any more.

"Ready for the big send-off, Ethan?" grinned Jackie as she came over. She wiped her forehead with her sleeve. "Pretend we've just gone for a cruise down the canal. We'll always be on the water in spirit."

Jackie wrapped her arms around him and squeezed him tight. "Come and see us, Ethan. Thank you. You've been such a good friend to Polly." Ethan's eyes felt prickly with tears now.

Jackie climbed on to the stern. "I've got to pack up my candles," she said, and disappeared down into her bedroom.

"Come and see me," said Polly. "Come and stay at my house and we can talk."

He nodded. But what if he didn't talk again? Could he speak without Polly? Then his arms were around Polly and her hair was soft against his neck and her skin smelt like buttermilk pancakes. He didn't want to let go.

Polly stepped back.

"Bye, Ethan," she said. Her eyes glistened, but she smiled.

He wiped his cheek with his coat sleeve. He took a big breath to make him brave.

Polly climbed on to the roof. Jackie started the engine. Ethan undid the centre rope and threw it to Polly. She caught it, winding it into a tight circle on the roof. Jackie waited until the nose drifted out from the bank, then she engaged the throttle. Then they were gliding slowly past him, east down the canal, towards the long dark tunnel and his old tree house.

They turned back and waved.

"Bye," Polly called out, and the sound was carried to him on a soft breeze. He could see each letter spelt out in the air. He waved. Polly waved again. She kept waving until they were out of sight. His chest rose and fell like it was pumping the air from his mouth.

"Bye," Ethan said. The sound was so quiet he wasn't sure he'd made it.

"Bye," he said, louder now. The sound hummed in his ears and his throat and his mouth. And he didn't feel afraid.

CHAPTER 22

Ethan turned away from the water. *Moon's End's* ripples had gone now; he didn't know what to do next. Slowly he walked to *Deity*. He could try and say something to Dad or Mum, but he wasn't ready yet. Nodding and shaking his head was what he did. He'd keep his voice to himself for now.

"We'll take you to see Polly, I promise," said Mum when she came into his cabin after bedtime. She sat on the floor next to his bed. "Don't forget, Mary's coming to see you tomorrow."

Ethan had forgotten about Mary coming back.

He'd been so busy thinking about Dad and Polly. Now Polly had gone and Mary was coming back to talk about school but now he wasn't so scared.

"Ethan, I know you're upset about Polly, but don't go to the pond in the morning. Wait for Mary."

He nodded. Mum stood up and kissed the top of his head.

"OK. Sleep tight."

Merlin climbed on to his chest when Mum left. Ethan stroked her back and she started to purr. Did her voice hum in her ears just like his had? He kept stroking. Merlin meowed like she was talking, like she wanted him to speak to her. If he tried again now, no one would know.

"Merlin."

He'd spoken a little louder than last time, but still he didn't feel sick.

Merlin fixed him with her green eyes. She meowed.

"Merlin."

One of his tears fell on her fur.

"My wish came true."

CHAPTER 23

Ethan sat on the sofa. Mum and Dad sat next to him. Mum and Dad didn't say anything about real school as they waited for Mary. They didn't ask if he'd thought about it, or if he had decided what he wanted to do. The boat was quiet. Ethan's heart was beating the seconds away. Still no one knew he had spoken.

There was a knock on the bow doors at exactly nine o'clock. Mum went up the stairs. Mary's heels clacked on the wooden steps.

"Hello again, Ethan," she said. She took off her

coat and sat on the fold-out chair by the kitchen. "So, how are you? Did you finish your knight's journal?"

"Almost," said Mum as she sat. "He's been doing well in all his subjects. We're ahead of the schedule I planned."

"Well done, Ethan," said Mary. "I'm sorry if I surprised you last time. I didn't mean to frighten you by talking about school."

School. The word felt so strange.

"Coffee?" said Dad quickly. Mary nodded. Dad got up and put the kettle on. There was a clatter of cups in the kitchen.

"Ethan made a really good friend on the canal," said Mum. "A girl his age. But Polly moved on yesterday. He's a bit upset."

"I'm very sorry to hear that, Ethan. But I hear you've been using a notebook? What a wonderful idea. And you used it to speak to your friend?"

He nodded.

Dad handed Mary a cup. He sat back down.

Mum took Dad's hand. Ethan's heart felt like it was running away from him, but he didn't want to stand up or run off the boat, not yet.

"Ethan," said Dad softly. "All right?"

He didn't shake his head or make the rug slide.

"Are you OK to talk about this?" Mum put her hand on his shoulder.

He nodded.

"It's not that you can't be taught on the canal," said Mary, "we just want to discuss all the options." She put her cup on the floor. She started talking slowly, carefully, like each word might be one too many. Mum and Dad watched him closely. Dad still held Mum's hand.

"I met with Mr Cabot. He'd be really happy to show you his school."

Mum leant forward. "Wait. . ."

"It's OK, Caitlin," said Dad.

Ethan's palms were sticky. In the new tree house Polly had said he was bigger than the canal. She had said he could go further than the market and the library. That he could go back to school and it would be all right. Polly believed he'd speak again and he had – she'd been right.

"There's no pressure if you don't want to," said Mum.

Ethan thought for a moment. He took a big breath. His heart thudded. He nodded.

"Are you sure, Ethan?" said Mum.

"That's something you'd like to do?" asked Mary.

"Have a look," said Dad. "If you choose not to go, that's fine. We'll just see how it goes."

"I'll arrange a time with Mr Cabot," said Mary. "How's next week?"

"Fine," said Dad. "Any day, I'll take time off work."

"I'll call and let you know," said Mary. "If there's a problem or you have a question, you've got my number."

Mary stood up and put on her coat.

Dad put his arm around Ethan. "I'm proud of you, son," he said.

CHAPTER 24

"Ready?"

Ethan looked at Dad and his heart raced. He didn't want to go inside. He wished he hadn't said yes to Mary.

"It'll be fine, son. We'll just take a look. They know all about you."

Dad reached across Ethan and opened the van door. He smiled. "Out you get."

Ethan climbed out, but his legs were wobbly. They said he could make up his own mind once he'd visited. When they got home he'd write it on a piece of paper:

I changed my mind
I don't want to go to school.
I'm scared.
I'll get teased like before.

"Must be this way." Dad led Ethan across the car park, past a big sign saying **Reception**. They went through a glass door and into a little area with chairs. Dad went over to the lady at the desk. "I'll tell him you're here," she said.

They sat down. Two boys walked past them and turned down a long hallway. They wore red and blue clothes. Ethan's heart fluttered but they smiled at him as they went past. He stared out of the window at the concrete playground. He remembered the playground at his old school and shivered.

The door next to the desk swung open and a tall man with a brown beard came through it. "You must be Ethan," he smiled. "I'm Mr Cabot."

Ethan tried to smile back. Dad stood up, so he did too. Then Dad shook the man's hand. "Jake Meaden."

Ethan's palms were sweaty; he didn't want to shake Mr Cabot's hand.

"Thank you for coming," said Mr Cabot. "Let's start with the library."

194

They followed Mr Cabot past the desk, through a door and down the long corridor.

"We're not a big school," he said, "just a hundred and fifty pupils. I like it that way. It makes us really friendly."

The corridor walls were covered with project work: the Egyptians, rivers and the Victorians. They came to a door that said **Library** in coloured paper letters. Mr Cabot opened the door and they followed him inside: it was much smaller than the library in town.

"Take a look, Ethan," said Mr Cabot. "We've got a great range of books."

Ethan went to a shelf and looked at the book spines. Even though it was a smaller library, there were lots of books he hadn't read because they were always on loan.

There was a pile of coloured cushions in the corner of the room. Mr Cabot caught him looking. "That's our reading area. Our pupils sit down over there when they want some peace and quiet."

They left the library and went through a big room with a high ceiling and a wooden floor. "This is our hall and our lunchroom too. I'll take you outside."

The school was surrounded by fields.

"Look at that," said Dad.

There was a castle made from logs that you could climb up. It had a log bridge with chains at each side.

"A school with a castle, hey," said Dad.

"Do you want to see the conservation area, Ethan?" asked Mr Cabot.

Ethan nodded and they walked on.

There was a pond at the side of the school. The grass around the pond was overgrown like a canal bank.

"We get lots of wildlife," said Mr Cabot. "Tadpoles, frogs, fish. There's still some work to do. The children take it in turns to look after the pond."

Dad nodded. "Great."

They left the pond and the castle and went in to see the IT room. Then Mr Cabot stopped at a blue door.

"You can have a look in, Ethan, if you like," said Mr Cabot. "This is Miss Pimms' class for pupils your age."

Ethan looked at Dad and Dad put a hand on his shoulder. "You don't have to," he said gently.

Ethan nodded, but his heart began to race. He

could hear the teacher asking a question. Mr Cabot went in first, then Dad, then him.

"Mrs Pimms, I've got someone I'd like you to meet."

Dad stood behind Ethan and put both hands on his shoulders.

The teacher and all the red and blue children looked around at him. Ethan felt dizzy.

The teacher smiled. "Of course."

The walls were covered with sheets of coloured paper: big words and pictures.

"I've heard all about you, Ethan," the teacher smiled.

The red and blue children were still looking at him but lots were smiling now.

Mr Cabot bent down to Ethan and whispered, "We've got a big blank page here and a pen, if you wanted to introduce yourself." He pointed to a big white board on the wall at the front of the class. He took out a thick black pen from his pocket. "You don't have to write big letters."

School was more colourful than he had expected. There was a castle and water and a blank page; it wasn't so different from the canal after all.

Ethan looked at Dad. "Only if you want to," Dad said.

Ethan nodded. Mr Cabot led him through the tables to Miss Pimms at the front of the class.

He tried not to look at all the children sitting in front of him, watching. He tried to imagine it was just him and Polly, on the canal with his notebook.

"Whenever you're ready," Miss Pimms said.

Ethan turned to face the big white board. It was taller than he was. He pulled the lid off the pen. The classroom was quiet. He lifted the pen to the big white page and pressed the tip against it. His hand was shaky. Dad smiled and nodded. Ethan took the pen away from the board and put it on the metal shelf underneath. Dad's smile fell. Ethan looked out at Dad and all the boys and girls. He took a big breath to make him brave and he said, "I'm Ethan. I live on the canal."

EPILOGUE

Ethan scrolled down to the bottom of the journal;
Dad only had one entry left to read now.

A wonderful thing has happened:
I am a knight at last. I was the most terrified I have
ever been as I rode into battle. But I took a big
breath, I drew my sword from my scabbard
and I charged at the enemy.
I was knighted on the battlefield for an act
of great bravery. I was given my title.
I think I am going to like being a knight.

ABOUT THE AUTHOR

Rachel grew up on a Somerset smallholding surrounded by animals. At the age of twelve she was selected to attend a week-long creative writing course where she was in her element. Rachel now lives in Bristol where she works in a museum. This is her first book.